Chapter 1

Washington D.C.

Kristin turned the channel to CNN. The alien ambassador's speech was playing:

"Greetings, citizens of Earth, from Cordia II. We wish to fix your environment with our technology, so that your planet will last for many years to come. In exchange, we want fifty of your women. It is a small price to pay. I must return home today, but I have left a ship on your planet to transport the women to Cordia II. It is on autopilot and will not fail. The brides will have a safe and pleasant journey. I thank you for welcoming me, and we look forward to forming a kinship between our peoples."

Another old clip played. "I am so thrilled to be one of the chosen ones," the woman with the "Save the Whales" t-shirt said as if she had just made it to the final round of a Miss America contest. "It is a great honor to know that I am doing all that I can for my planet to make it truly green."

The TV anchor came back on in real time. "Well, there you have it, folks. Five women have been chosen to participate in the exchange until positive proof is given that they can and will fix our environment. The committee is still in session to determine final approval of the exchange. In other news—"

Kristin hit the off button on the remote with a vengeance. She believed in doing your part to save the planet as much as the next person, but this exchange that was going to take place was so medieval.

Kristin' father, the Secretary of Defense, was a part of the committee that was going to decide if it was a rational idea, and she anxiously waited for his return though it was long past the time she usually went to bed.

"Well?" she asked as soon as he came through the door.

"We have discussed it, and it was unanimous," he said, dark circles under his weathered face. "If they can truly do what they claim, it is worth doing the exchange."

"Why am I not surprised? Politicians stamping all over human rights. It's not exactly a new thing, is it?"

"It's not as if we will be kidnapping women off the street and making them go. They will all volunteer for the mission."

"Only because they don't know any better. What happens if they change their mind when they get there? Will they be allowed to come back?"

He was slow to answer. "I'm sure if they—"

"But you don't know," she interrupted. She picked up her purse.

"Where are you going this time of night?" he demanded as if she were not twenty-five but fifteen. "You can stay over."

"I'm doing what you taught me, being a political activist. It may be too late to write my congressman, but it may not be too late for some of the women."

***

Kristin waited for the right opportunity, and when the guards were engaged in conversation with each other, she slipped past them toward the spaceship.

Kristin saw the five women waiting on the platform next to it. They'd had a lot of publicity in the past couple of days.

The Save-The-Whales woman was there. The woman beside her wore square, black frames, the astrologist. One of the woman was applying lipstick in the reflection from the metal ship. She didn't remember what her profession was, but by the way she was dressed, it was clear the thrill for her lay in marrying an alien to put it mildly. One was an older woman, who must have thought this was her last chance to get married and have children. The last was a shy-looking girl, who looked like she thought the same thing, although she was still quite young.

Kristin planned to try and talk them all out of it, but she realized her best chance was the shy one as she stood off from the other, looking a tad unsure.

She immediately started talking to her as soon as she got onto the platform. "Hi, I'm Kristin Harvey. I have a question for you. Why? You don't know what these aliens are like. What if they're cannibals? What if they're a sexist society? Do you know anything about their culture other than the fact that they have a bunch of fancy gadgets?"

Her confidence was undermined right away. "No, I guess I don't."

"So why are you throwing your life away for the unknown?"

"I—I don't really know."

A voice came over the speakers. "Please, get into the ship. Takeoff will be in ten minutes."

Kristin was desperate. "There's still time to escape, time to save yourself. Do you really want to leave the only home you've ever known, your family, your friends?"

She vigorously shook her head and took off in the direction away from the ship, half walking and half running.

The others had already gone onto the ship. Kristin sighed a sigh that was half relief and half disappointment. At least she'd had one victory. She started to leave the platform, but one of the guards, who came to check that the platform was clear, saw her.

"Why aren't you on the ship? The ship is getting ready to leave. Are the other girls on board?"

"Four of them are. One of them changed her mind," she said proudly.

His eyebrows furrowed angrily as he realized that she was the one who had helped change her mind. "Do you know where I was born?" he asked her. "In Los Angeles. Smog just settles in the air, and there's not enough rain to wash it away. Now I admit that pollution has been dropping, but it's still out of control. I am not going to jeopardize the chance for a pollution-free world. If you talked a bride into leaving, you can just take her place."

Before Kristin knew what was happening, she was shoved onto the ship and the door was locked with a loud noise behind her. She banged on the door and yelled for someone to let her out, but she knew nobody could hear her over the sound of the engines beginning to fire up.

Chapter 2

"It won't be so bad," the older woman attempted to reassure her.

They were hurdling through space, and it wasn't the speed making her feel nauseous, but the thought of what might happen when they arrived.

The astrologist was trying to catch a glimpse of their travels through the small window even though they were moving too fast for that as if this were all a lark.

Kristin scoffed. "Do you think they will allow me to return when I tell them what happened?"

The women were pointedly silent. They had no more of an idea than her father had. They had made introductions over the course of the last hour. Maggie was the environmentalist, Ruth was the astrologist, Brittney was the scantily clad woman, and LeAnn was the older woman.

"It's strange we're not all sick traveling at this speed," said Brittney, attempting to change the subject.

"Well, we are traveling so fast you cannot get sick," Ruth explained, turning around to answer the question. "It doesn't even feel as if we are moving, does it? You see—"

"Whoa," Brittney interrupted, holding her hands up in mock surrender. "No need for fancy explanations. I was just making an observation."

The rest of the trip was mostly quiet as they all contemplated their futures.

They could feel the change in gravity when they hit the small planet's atmosphere. They knew that they'd reached Cordia II. They landed, and an alien opened the door for them.

Kristin was stunned by the scenery. The buildings looked like ice palaces though it was very warm weather; it was like being in a strange winter wonderland. But the most beautiful part was three white-faced moons that shone down from the darkening sky. It was like being inside a fantastical painting.

They were on a raised platform. A large crowd surrounded them made up of mostly men. The alien, who had let them out, stayed on the platform with them. He addressed the crowd in English to accommodate the visitors.

She wondered if their form was to accommodate them as well. Maybe they really looked like squids. She was pretty sure she had seen that in a sci-fi movie once.

"If you do not get a woman today, do not be worried. There will be more to come once they see we are a people of out word. We shall start with this fine-looking Earth woman," he said, gesturing toward Ruth.

Kristin realized this was their auctioneer of sorts. She felt like a part of a herd of cattle being auctioned. The men did look hungry but not for beef. Although the way most of them were staring, the more accurate comparison might have been the way a wine collector stared at a collection of rare bottles. Why had they wanted women in exchange anyway?

She noticed one man in particular leering at her while the others were auctioned. He clearly intended to bid on her and win.

For a moment, she thought about running, but there was nowhere to hide on a strange planet. Surely they were a reasonable people. When her turn came, she told the auctioneer, "I am not here freely; I was kidnapped. I would like to return to Earth."

He looked at her as if mulling it over and then continued as if she hadn't said anything. She was about to become the leering man's possession any minute now.

***

"I don't approve of this," Moz'us said to his father.

"There is no other way, and you don't have to choose a bride this time. Forty-five more women will be here soon." He chuckled. "You have to give them credit for their shrewdness. There was a time when their suspicions may have been justified if they had dealt with our ancestors."

"Are we repairing their atmosphere as we speak?"

He nodded. "Yes, but only ten percent of it until we get the others. Their own history is not always one of honesty or fairness."

"How are we or they to find happiness? They're being sold like property. We know nothing of them beyond their looks and the fact that we are genetically compatible."

"Unfortunately, happiness is not the primary concern right now. Seeing that Cordia II survives is. That means taking a wife and ensuring that the race, and our bloodline, does not die out."

Moz'us sighed. It always went back to duty with his father and ensuring that Cordia II's rich history lasted.

He was caught off guard by the woman who was getting sold at the moment. She didn't appear to be enjoying being here. In fact, she looked angry from the top of her brunette locks down to the tips of her toes, which made her beauty more pointed.

***

The price for her had become ridiculously high. She knew that because the other bidders were dropping out. She looked over the audience, hoping for another bidder. Right now she'd settle for any of them besides Mr. Lecher over there.

She caught his eyes for just a moment. This particular alien looked kind, uncomfortable with these proceedings, and not hard on the eyes at all. Even from the platform, she could tell that he had amazing blue-green eyes that contrasted with nearly jet-black hair. If only he was bidding, she might not mind so much. Well, that wasn't true, she would mind, but maybe he would free her.

"I'll take her to wife!" shouted Blue-Eyes suddenly and fervently.

Then again, she thought, maybe she was wrong about her quick judgment.

***

Everything instantly became quiet. Moz'us was the son of one of the ruling members. If he wanted one of the brides, he did not have to outbid competitors.

"Then may Kralgiek bless your union," said the auctioneer, regaining his voice. He was surprised by his bid.

"He does not intend to bed her!" shouted Scrak'uils. He was upset because he'd almost won her. But Moz'us wouldn't wish any woman on him. He couldn't do anything about the future, but he could save the spirited lady, who was now glaring daggers at him.

Moz'us frowned at him. It was true. He didn't want to marry a stranger, and he doubted the woman he'd chosen wanted to marry him either.

"Do you have proof of this claim, Scrak'uils?" asked Xuq'eots. He was the head of the ruling class, and the people around him moved back to create a small circular space around him.

"Everyone knows it to be true. As the head, Xuq'eots, you should as well. Moz'us has been against this idea from the beginning. How many times have we had to listen to his romantic ideas about what love and marriage should be? He expected us to travel there and find a woman to come back with us. As if we had time to devote to their primitive courtship. Now he find it suitable to his tastes?"

Xuq'eots nodded. "What you say is true, but he is a man who surely wants children. He has the right to choose a bride, despite his earlier opposition."

"That is my point, your honor. I am not sure that he has changed his mind. Should we allow a man to take a wife if he does not intend to use her? Bearing Cordia II's next generation is the primary goal in this. What if he doesn't seek to take her to his bed but considers himself to be a hero rescuing this 'poor' girl. I would be surprised to see their ceremony at all."

"What do you have to say to that, Moz'us?" Xuq'eots asked.

"I'll tell you what I have to say," she said, speaking up. "I am not going to anyone's bed but my own. I am not some animal to be bred. Return me to Earth."

"I say that I do intend to marry and produce offspring with her. I have accepted the decision that was made and have seen the wisdom in it," Moz'us answered.

"That is good enough for me," Xuq'eots said.

"What about me? Don't I get a say in this?" she still demanded from the platform.

"However to satisfy Scrak'uils, your wedding will take place immediately," said Xuq'eots with finality in his voice. "If a few months show no fruit from your union, there will be inquiry. A few men will still be without wives when these proceedings are over. Fifty was all they would allow. It would be unfair for you to have a wife if you do not intend to use her in the capacity of a wife."

Moz'us swallowed hard. "I understand, sir."

"What does it take for you to understand that I want to go home?" she said loudly but slowly as if she were speaking to imbeciles. "I never wanted to come here! What happens if I refuse to marry this Moz'us person?".

"Then you may choose Scrak'uils," Xuq'eots replied calmly, finally acknowledging her presence. "We would take your opinion into consideration."

"How about no one?"

He firmly shook his head. "That is not an option, I'm afraid. You are here now. You must stay here."

She was the last of the brides. The crowd got noisy as they began to disperse, probably discussing all the excitement.

"I hope that you truly wanted to marry her," his father said to him quietly. "There is no way to get out of it now. I will walk ahead to give you two a chance to get to know each other. With luck, you will be able to calm and reassure her about her future."

He would need more than luck. He waited patiently for her to come down off of the platform, but when he saw that she didn't intend to go anywhere, he went up to her.

Chapter 3

"We have to go now," Moz'us said, "and I'm sure you are hungry after your long trip."

Kristin was hungry. Staying on the platform all day wouldn't help anything. She followed him down the stairs. "You know, I've kept a reign on my tongue up until now because I don't really know what you people are like or how your government works, but if you think—"

"You've kept a reign on your tongue?" he asked. He looked genuinely puzzled. She had spoken more than once in protest. His look said he'd hate to see her tongue without a reign on it.

That question infuriated her even more. He ducked the pocketbook that she hurled at him. He had no idea what he had gotten himself into.

"What do you intend to do with me when we get there?" she asked.

He looked at her in surprise. "Feed you, I guess. I'm sure my mother is preparing something for your arrival. My father left before us and will tell her about you I am sure."

"You live with your parents?"

"There isn't enough land to expand on. We have to live in the buildings we have."

"Of course, I didn't think about that." It had looked much smaller than Earth from the window. "So how is it that you know English anyway?"

"We have been considering this for some time. It only made sense we learned the language of the people we intended to wed. Some of us visited your planet long before we approached your planet with the idea."

Kristin came to a complete stop, her mouth hanging open, "What?"

"We blend in perfectly. It's not like we're little green men."

"You mean you look like this all the time?"

He grinned. "Did you think we were wearing costumes?"

She looked indignant. "No, but I mean you could have transformed yourself."

"Not unless you know something we don't. There are other planets where—"

"There is life on other planets as well.

"Of course. The universe is vast."

"Right," she said and started walking again. "And in this vast universe, the resource you wanted most is women from our planet. Makes sense."

"We destroyed our first planet in much the same way your people is destroying theirs. That's why there's a II in our planet's name. We found a habitable empty planet and used our technology to rebuild as much as possible. Unfortunately, a new planet was hard on our women and girls before we got the atmosphere just right, and a lot of them died. Your planet is the closet one to ours and the most genetically similar. We had a hard time choosing a language. There are so many on your planet. In the end, English was chosen. Those who are my age and younger learned it as children."

It was astonishing to think this had been in the works for that long. They had been sure of their plan working. She couldn't help finding all this new information fascinating in spite of herself. "How many languages do your people have?"

"Just one. We speak that too at times, but we are making an effort to use English more often for your sakes."

"Hmm," she said. Courteous considering they were ripping them from the only life they had ever known.

"Do you mind if I ask a question now?" he asked. He remembered the flying object that had almost hit him in the head.

"Sure." It sounded like they already knew everything about Earth. She wonder what he could possibly want to know.

"What's your name?"

"Kristin," she answered slowly. If he had any designs about winning her over with his other worldly charm, he could forget it. She still didn't trust him or anybody else on this planet.

They fell to an uncomfortable silence until Moz'us stopped walking.

"This is it?" she asked, looking up at the crystal structure that loomed before them.

"This is it," he affirmed. He sounded nervous as he asked, "Do—do you like it?"

"It'll do. I don't plan to be here for long." She went in before he could ask her what she meant by that.

True to his prediction, his mother had made her something to eat. It looked like a hamburger. She was smiling warmly at her. "I'm Es'a. Welcome to your new home. I've made one of your delicacies on Earth."

"And I'm Ix'els," his father said. "Welcome."

"Thank you," Kristin said warily as she sat down. She took a bite out of the sandwich. She did her best not to make a face of disgust, out of politeness and because she didn't know how they would react if they took offense.

She wondered how something that looked so much like a hamburger could taste so different from a hamburger. "It's delicious," she told the eagerly waiting woman.

Es'a smiled in relief. "I'm glad." Ix'els said something to his wife, and they left the room.

"Would you like some?" Kristin asked Moz'us, hoping to split the sandwich with him to half the torture.

"No, thank you. I already ate. I have some things I need to take care of. Make yourself at home, and I'll be back shortly."

She watched him leave the house. Then she looked back to the makeshift hamburger. She was starving. As much as she hated to, she forced herself to finish it all. It would provide nutrition, or so she hoped.

She took a closer look at her surroundings. The room was not cluttered with knickknacks or anything else that did not have an obvious purpose. It was evident that this was a society that was founded on usefulness and not emotion, which made sense when one thought about how they got their brides in the first place.

She got up and took a walk around the nearly empty space and heard Ix'els and Es'a talking in another room. She was sure the "make yourself at home" did not extend to eavesdropping on his parents, but she had to learn as much as possible about this place, so she could make a proper escape.

"I am glad that he has chosen a bride," Es'a said. "I was afraid that he wouldn't."

"I just hope that he has chosen well. The ship will leave in two weeks to retrieve the other women. He should have waited for more selection."

"Why two weeks?"

"Their scientists want time to evaluate the results."

Kristin walked away before she was caught. She was thankful they were making an effort to speak English even amongst themselves; she had heard what she needed to know. When that ship left to get the other brides, she planned to be on it.

Chapter 4

Kristin had grown tired of exploring the house and was retracing her way back to the platform in her mind. She didn't know if she would be allowed to see light of day again, and she had to keep the directions clear in her mind.

"Where were you?" she asked when Moz'us finally returned.

He smiled. "You already sound like a suspicious wife."

"I am simply curious to know if it was about anything having to do with me."

"It was actually. I was hoping that I could find a loophole for you. I know you're not thrilled with this arrangement."

"And?"

"I wasn't successful, but I did learn that our wedding ceremony will take place tomorrow at midday."

"Yippee," she said sarcastically. "And there's nothing else to be done?"

"I'm afraid not," he said sympathetically. "I understand why you're not happy about this. If it helps, I am not in agreement with the idea either. I do like you from our short acquaintance, but I wish we knew each other better."

She softened a little toward him. He was trying to help her. He wasn't as bad as the rest of them. "There's something else I want to know. Does your mother always fix hamburgers?"

"You sure ask a lot of questions," he said with an amused expression.

"So I've been told. Are you going to answer me?"

"I could tell it was not your favorite, but I want to thank you for being kind to my mother."

"Well, I don't think she was trying to poison me. Was she?"

"No," he answered chuckling.

"I'm just glad the water tasted like real water."

"Our food is different from what you eat on Earth. She was trying out something you might enjoy and make you feel more at home, unsuccessful thought it might have been."

"So your mother is a good cook," she said. "That is a relief." She didn't want that kind of fare the whole two weeks she was here. She might starve to death before she ever made it to the ship.

"How could she not be? How could anyone be a bad cook?" he asked as if it would be hard to ruin a meal.

"It's very easy," she answered, recalling all the times she had effortlessly created disasters in the kitchen.

Recognition filled his eyes. "I'm sorry. I forgot you do it by hand on Earth. Here we have a device that will make food for you simply by thinking about it. The hamburger probably wasn't good because my mother didn't have a clear idea on what a hamburger is supposed to taste like. I'm sure if you ask, she'll let you try it, so you'll have better results."

Kristin was amazed and seriously contemplating taking one with her when she went back to Earth.

"Do you mind if I question you now?" he asked. "How were you kidnapped?"

She didn't really want to talk about it, but he had complied with her questions; it was only fair that she answered his. "I managed to talk one of the brides out of coming here, so one of the guards pushed me into the ship to take her place."

"Do your women often get into such trouble?"

She folded her arms. "No, they do not."

"Do you?"

She refused to dignify the question with an answer. Although truth be told, the answer to that question was yes. Her activist ways did frequently get her into trouble. "I think the whole practice is barbaric and disgusting. We've lost a couple of centuries of progress by treating women as bargaining chips."

"Why? It is not unheard of in your world."

"Maybe not, but it's unheard of in America."

"What about tobacco brides?" he asked.

"Tobacco what?"

"When there weren't enough women in the colonies, they brought over women, sometimes willingly and sometimes not, from England in exchange for tobacco. Whatever your feelings, you must admit the environment is a more worthy exchange than tobacco, and ideally the brides should have been all ones who were willing to come. That was the plan."

"Okay, that's one example," she conceded.

"And mail-order brides in the Old West," he supplied. "Not enough women in that part of the country, so they sent advertisements for them."

She had heard of that practice. "How do you know all this?" she asked.

"We had to study Earth history in school. I don't everything about your planet, but I know a lot."

Now that it was completely dark, she went over to the window to look out. She still couldn't believe she was here. She watched as the white-faced moons shone over the landscape, making the buildings sparkle and the stars grow even more vivid and beautiful than she ever thought possible due to all the extra light.

"Come with me, dear," Es'a said, breaking in on the wonder, "and I'll show you to your room. You will not share Moz'us' room until after the ceremony."

Kristin breathed a sigh of release to know she was getting her own room. At least, there would be no consummating their relationship tonight or ever if she could help it.

Es'a looked in Moz'us' direction. "I hope you've gotten a chance to get to know each other a little bit."

"I think so," he answered.

They had gotten to know each other better, but Moz'us shot her a private look that said he knew it would take many more days to work out the enigma that was Kristin Harvey. Longer than she would be here.

Chapter 5

Kristin arrived at the place where she and Moz'us were to be married. Es'a was the only one accompanying her.

In the room where the ceremony would happen, she took a step back, startled. Above where the minister would likely stand was a gigantic painting. On one half was Ix'els and Es'a and on the other side was a faceless male and female, but they wore Earth clothes and not the silvery, reflective robes that were worn here. "What in the world..." Kristin began.

"We were not sure what your parents looked like," Es'a quickly explained. When that didn't seem to dispel her confusion, Es'a realized she was confused about the picture itself. "It's an old Cordian custom symbolizing the uniting of two families."

"Oh, I guess that makes sense."

Es'a peered critically at her image. "I don't think they captured my likeness."

Kristin thought it looked very accurate except that the eyes were lifeless. It was completely devoid of any emotions. On second thought, maybe it was just one more testament to how these people were.

She was ushered into a large room. "This is where you will change and await the ceremony." There was a thin box sitting on a table. Es'a pulled the lid off and lifted a wedding dress out of it. "This is the dress that I married Ix'els in, and I want you to wear it."

"Thank you," she said. As much as she was against this wedding, it was a nice gesture to show that she didn't despise her son's alien bride.

"I'll step out and give you a chance to get it on," Es'a said.

Kristin eyed herself in the mirror after she got it on. In the wedding dress, she looked like one of them. It was a white dress covered in sparkling crystals, but it had a space-age look to it. It was also very modest. The only visible part of her was her face and the upper part of her neck thanks to gloves, veil, and a very long hemline.

She hadn't heard the door open again and a figure joined her in the mirror's reflection. "You look lovely, my dear. This will be a good marriage, you'll see."

Kristin did her best not to scoff. That was easy for her to say. It was her son, and his marriage prospects had been minimal before the brides from Earth had arrived if he wasn't willing to wait.

Time certainly didn't drag in Kristin's mind. It didn't seem like long before the ceremony began. There was no formal walk down the aisle with music playing for the bride. She was grateful for that. Instead, she was lifted up onto a suspended platform with Moz'us and the minister.

Instead of rings, they had necklaces. Kristin admired them. They were identical and very beautiful. "No one can duplicate this color pattern," Moz'us explained to her in a whisper. "There has never been a pair like these and never will be again. It is registered in our names."

Kristin could barely hear the words of the ceremony. She was so stunned that this was happening to her, but she didn't believe it to be binding. She would be a free woman again on Earth.

She mumbled a yes when she sensed that they were waiting for an answer. Although if she had said no, it wouldn't have mattered.

"And now let the maid, Kristin Harvey, exchange the wedding necklaces with her spouse, Moz'us, citizen of Cordia II."

They put the necklaces over each other's heads and that was the end of the ceremony.

There was a party after the wedding with food and drink and music. That part was at least familiar to her even if the food, drink, and music were not. As the party wound down, she suddenly found herself getting pushed to the front of the crowd along with Moz'us.

"What's going on?" she whispered.

"It is time for the walk to the ceremonial bed."

"They come with us?" she asked alarmed.

He smiled. "Just to the door."

It wasn't a long walk back to the house. There were very few long walks in Cordia II, or at least in this city. You could see from one end of it to the other. She looked back a couple of times to see if the crowd was still behind them. They followed them right up to Moz'us's bedroom door.

Moz'us shut the door once they were inside. Her heartbeat sped up as she realized that she was alone with her newly wedded alien husband.

There was an uncomfortable silence as they looked at each other, wondering what would come next.

"So how do you—you know—" Kristin began at last.

"How do I what?" he asked.

She rolled her eyes. Was it possible that he was this naive? "When two people get together on their wedding night and—"

"Oh," he said, cutting her off, finally comprehending what she was talking about. "Well, I've never done it before. I only have a vague idea of how it's done."

"Is it different from the way we do it on Earth?"

He smiled his nervousness. "I don't think it's different."

Her eyes lowered and his cheeks became flushed as he all but read her thoughts. "Only our molecular structure is different. As I told you before, we are able to reproduce; that's why your planet was chosen."

"That doesn't mean there couldn't be a weird way of reproducing."

"I am sure that it's done the same way or I would have been told."

Another more uncomfortable silence settled.

Moz'us was the first to speak this time. "We'll have to do it at some point because they were serious about making sure we're married in every sense, but it doesn't have to be tonight."

Kristin was beyond relieved. "Thank you."

She looked around. It was a very simple room like all the other rooms. There was a bed and a closet and the scheme was done in white or silver, the favorite colors of Cordia II. Hanging in the closet next to

Moz'us' clothes were her Earth clothes and a nightgown that she had been given the night before. Her purse was hanging in there too.

"I'll turn around if you want, so you can change into your nightdress."

Kristin almost protested, not believing that he wouldn't look, but she realized that he could have forced himself on her if he had really wanted to. So while he was turned, she changed quickly.

She went over to the corner of the bed and sat down, tired of standing. She brought her pocketbook with her. She wanted to check and make sure everything was still there. Moz'us sat down on the other corner of the bed. He stared at her bag with interest.

She dumped the contents of her purse out onto the bed. This was all that she had from Earth except for the clothes that she had been wearing. There was half a roll of mints, her coin purse, her driver's license, her credit cards, two family pictures, a pen and notepad, her cell phone, and her keys. She searched the inside of her purse to be sure that was it and found a discarded movie ticket.

"What are these?" he said, pointing to the mints.

"I thought you said you studied Earth history?"

"History and culture studies, but that doesn't mean it covered everything or that I remember everything."

She pulled one of them out of the wrapper. "You suck on it, and it helps your breath smell better. Do you want one?"

"Are you trying to say that I have bad breath?" he asked teasingly.

"It never hurts to ensure that your bed companion has had a mint before he goes to bed," she teased back.

He took the mint. "And what does this device do?" he asked, picking up the cell phone.

"It's a phone to call people with."

"I thought so. Why didn't you call someone to let them know you were in the ship?"

"You don't think I thought of that? I forgot to charge it up, and I doubt there would have been any service, especially when the ship took off like a bat out of hell or maybe a bat going to hell would be more accurate."

He ignored the jab at his home. "That's obviously your money," he said, pointing to the coins. "What are the cards for?"

"This says I can drive," she said, putting the license back into the purse. "Sometimes I wonder if it's possible to get a decent picture on a driver's license. And these," she said as she picked up the credit cards, "allow me to buy without money."

"So you're allowed to buy with what you do not have?" he asked.

"Until your heart's content or you go bankrupt, whichever comes first."

"These are primitive ways to write," he said, looking at the pen and notepad.

"Excuse me?" she asked.

He looked flustered, "I didn't mean you were primitive, I—"

She interrupted him, "Don't worry, they're almost primitive on Earth too." She picked up her keys. "And these allow me to open my house, car, etcetera. We have scanning technology, but not for the everyday person and building." She put her keys back in and picked up the ticket. "This is what I went to see at the movies last, *The Alien's Bride*. Ironic, isn't it? And these are just pictures."

"May I see the pictures?" he asked.

She slowly handed them over. "The man is my dad, the woman is my mother, and I'm the baby."

"You were a cute baby," he said with a grin. His smile disappeared. "I bet your parents are worried about you."

"Not likely. My mother is dead, and my father is a career man more than a family man. It may be years before he notices that I'm missing."

He gave her the picture, and she put it carefully back in. "And this is my little sister. Everyone says she's the pretty one. I bet you wish that she was the one that had been kidnapped instead of me."

"Not really," he said, handing it back to her. "I suppose we should be getting into bed now. We'll have to share the bed. The floor is hard and cold, and the sheets are too thin to camp on it."

"The bed is big enough for the both of us."

Once they were settled onto the bed, she asked, "So is everyone forced to marry someone they don't love?"

"We are not an overly romantic people if that's what you mean, and yet, there are some couples who manage to find love."

"So it's not easy for your people to fall in love?"

"I didn't say that, but we have pride in our sciences, and people often think in terms of matches rather than love."

"Were your parents one of the couples who fell in love?"

"Yes."

There was more quiet. They both were rather tense laying next to each other in the dark.

Moz'us said, "I hope you weren't offended by Ms. Kete-Re, the lady who was going around making snide remarks about people from Earth at the reception. I feel sorry for her future daughter-in-law."

"No worries." Kristin imitated her whiny voice, "These earth creatures are not worthy to wear our garments. They will think their selves our equals."

They both laughed hard at the spot-on impersonation, and it loosened the tension.

Kristin almost told him her plans to get back to Earth. He was obviously in agreement with her that this marriage shouldn't have taken place, but she came to her senses just in time. Just because he was friendlier than she had supposed didn't mean that he didn't feel more loyalty to his own people.

Chapter 6

The three Cordians watched as Kristin finished the last of her maple donuts and drank the last of her coffee. They stared at her as if they couldn't believe what she had just ate and drank it.

"It's not bad really," she said when she noticed their looks. "In fact, it's amazing. That machine works really well. It was like eating the best donut or drinking the best coffee I ever had all over again."

Moz'us' parents nodded to show that they were listening, but it didn't look as if they believed that it really tasted as good as she claimed.

"I hope you two have come to an understanding," Ix'els said, changing the subject. It was a friendly statement, but it was laced with a warning that the ruling class meant business.

"I think we have gotten to know each other better," Moz'us told him. It was the truth, not what Ix'els was looking for, but the truth. If the night had gone differently, their relationship could have been the worse for it.

Ix'els and Es'a seemed satisfied with that statement and went on with their morning.

"Where are your parents going?" Kristin asked once they'd left.

"My father is a part of the ruling class. They'll want to discuss how the exchange is going. My mother will also tell them about how the arrangement is working out."

"And of course, they won't ask the actual brides." Her eyes turned toward the door leading to the outside. "It must be nice to see the light of day," she mumbled, "even if the light is a small, white sun." She longed for all the colors her sun appeared to be when looking at it from Earth.

"You're not a prisoner," he told her with amusement.

"I'm not?" she asked with raised eyebrows.

"At least, you're not under house arrest," he rephrased.

She ventured toward the door and looked back to see if he was going to try and stop her. He made no move to get up from the table.

She stepped outside and took a deep breath. Being outside didn't make her feel any freer.

She didn't know where she was going, but she started walking. She had ten more days after today before the ship would take off for Earth. She might as well see everything there was to see in the meantime. This was a once in a lifetime experience.

One thing that she wasn't to fond of was that all the buildings were so similar, pretty though they were. It was like being in suburbia, only worse. However, on closer examination after she'd passed about a dozen, she saw that the buildings were different from one another. Some had a different number of windows, some had carvings. It just took studying them for a little while.

The street she was on at that moment wasn't very crowded, but when she turned the corner, it was suddenly teaming with life like a semi-respectable city.

She came to a complete stop when she saw one of the brides with her new husband. It was Ruth, the astrologist. He would point and talk, and she would take notes like a proper scientist. Kristin was positive that it wouldn't last. Once she learned all there was to know in this galaxy, she would want to return home.

Ruth wasn't the only bride she ran into, who was out honeymooning. LeAnn and her husband were looking more at each other than anything else.

Kristin was not enjoying this walk and turned around to head back. Besides, she didn't think it would look too good if she ran into someone and they reported that she was not spending time with Moz'us when they hadn't even been married for twenty-four hours yet.

She made a mental note to check on the other two brides. Surely one of them had discovered that life wasn't greener on the other side of the universe and that men were men wherever they were.

When the house came in sight, she saw that Moz'us must have been watching for her as he held the door open. She took a small step back in her surprise. She was unused to anyone waiting for her. She came and left her apartment on Earth when she pleased. The only living creatures she had to answer to if she was not at home were the fish and even they didn't seem to know when she was there or not. They swam around their bowl with or without her. They only noticed when there were specks of food sprinkled at the top of their bowl.

"Were you waiting on me?" she asked, puzzled.

"I was worried. I was getting ready to come look for you. I thought you might have gotten lost."

"Not likely," she said with a small scoff. "There's not much room to get lost in." She didn't know how anyone could live in such a small space. You could spend your whole life on Earth exploring and never see every square inch. In Cordia II, you'd be done in a matter of days.

"Our city is comparable to your city, Washington D.C.," he said. "Isn't that where you live? That's what your driver's license says."

"Yes, but it's different. I do have to admit that your buildings aren't highly varied. I would have had to think which house it was, so thanks for standing outside."

"You're welcome. Did you enjoy your walk?" he asked in a pleasant voice.

"Sure. A walk in the prison yard always lifts my sprits," came her sarcastic retort.

He looked more than a little disappointed that his attempt at light conversation had failed.

She wondered why he was so anxious to be friendly with her. Then she realized that as far as he knew, they would be stuck together for many years to come. "It wasn't that bad. After all, I have to get used to all this, don't I?"

She felt bad about the small white lie, but she was sure her leaving was what they both wanted.

***

The day dragged slowly after that because conversation was so stilted and she didn't have work with which to occupy herself, but it ended at last, and Kristin and Moz'us found themselves in bed again.

They lay there, wondering which would come first sleep or the need for conversation.

"How and why exactly does the ruling class plan to see if we have consummated our marriage?" she asked at last. She had tried to picture how they would test to determine that and none of the options she could think of were pretty.

"Well, the purpose of this exchange was not for companionship but to keep our race from dying out as you already know. That means they will be making sure that we and all the couples really are producing children and taking corrective measures if we're not."

"I see, so they will thoroughly examine us to find out why we're not having children, and it would become obvious if we hadn't consummated the relationship."

"Yes, but our methods are not as intrusive as they are on Earth. You will merely be scanned with a machine. You don't even have to remove any clothing."

That didn't keep it from feeling intrusive. "And when exactly do they plan to do this?"

"They will check after a month is up to see if you're pregnant, and if they discover that we haven't even made attempts in that direction, we could both be in serious trouble."

"How serious?"

"I don't suggest that we find out."

"Oh." Luckily, she wouldn't be there for that test. "That's rather harsh though, isn't it?"

"Not if you think of it in practical terms. They are ensuring that there will be Cordians in the future."

"That's what I mean. It doesn't leave very much room for individual human feeling, does it?"

"No."

She couldn't help but wonder where he stood on the subject. According to what she had heard from the man whose bride she had almost become, Moz'us had argued against the bridal exchange. Did he side against checking to see if the couples were having children too? She had a feeling he didn't like it any better than she did, especially since he hadn't insisted on working toward that goal tonight.

"Goodnight, Kristin."

It felt ridiculous to her to say goodnight to someone before going to sleep. It's not like she was going anywhere. Even when she had lived at home, it wasn't a tradition that her family had observed.

He repeated it again. "Goodnight, Kristin."

She wavered. It may have been a stupid tradition, but she was getting sleepy and she had a feeling he would not stop until he got his goodnight, "Goodnight, Moz'us."

Chapter 7

Moz'us and Kristin had been abandoned at the breakfast table once more, and Kristin didn't think it was by coincidence. Ix'els and Es'a hadn't been very subtle about it. They were doing their best to let them enjoy a honeymoon period.

"So do you know where all the brides went?" she asked, hoping she sounded casual.

He looked mildly taken aback at first, but he answered, "I know their husbands."

"Can you show me where they live?"

"I can," he said, "or I can give you directions."

It was Kristin's turn to be astonished. He was making it so easy for her. "Directions would be great."

He brought an electronic device to the table and began typing in information.

"Are you terribly lonely?" he asked in a quiet voice as he handed over the GPS-like device to her.

"If you were on Earth and there were only four other of your people, wouldn't you seek them out?"

"I guess I would," he conceded. "And you want to see if they're happy with the arrangement, don't you?"

She was shocked by how much he was learning about her. It was unsettling. "It's just idle curiosity."

He looked as if he believed that it was more than idle, but he didn't question her further, and she hurried out the door.

Maggie, the environmentalist, answered the door of the first house.

"May I speak to you outside?" Kristin posed.

Maggie nodded and followed her out.

"Are you happy?" Kristin asked, getting right down to business.

"I'm content," she answered. "The fact that I still get to eat what I want was a nice surprise. It will take some adjustment getting used to the new culture, but it's not a bad one. Just different."

"But do you love your husband?"

"I didn't expect it to be love at first sight, but I will not jeopardize the arrangement. I am doing this for the environment. I do like him though. We're getting to know each other better. Who knows? One day I may learn to love him."

Kristin sighed in frustration. "So if you had the chance to escape back to Earth, figuratively speaking, you wouldn't take it?"

"I wouldn't even be tempted."

"Well, I guess I'll be seeing you around. I just wanted to know how it was going for you."

Kristin knew that Maggie was yet another one she could mark off the list. If the last bride was happy, it looked like she would be going back by herself.

Brittney was sitting outside her home, alone. She had a miserable look plastered on her face. Kristin couldn't help but be pleased by it. Here was a chance to help.

"You don't look very happy. Isn't married life treating you well?" she asked.

"It's nothing like I expected. Oh sure, the wedding night wasn't so bad, but it's been downhill from there."

"Then come back to Earth with me. This isn't the Middle Ages. We have rights."

"How can we go back to Earth?"

Kristin didn't want to give her the details. She couldn't take a chance on the plan becoming known. "I have an idea that I know will work. You just have to agree to it."

"I'll think about it," she said slowly.

Kristin was satisfied with the answer for now. After all, Brittney still had nine days left to think about it. "Good. I'll talk to you more later."

She walked back to her temporary home with a smile, and she was still smiling when she came through the door.

"That was fast. Did you have a nice time?" Moz'us asked.

"I did. I had a good chat."

"You like going out, don't you?"

"It's better than being stuck in this fortress all day."

He smiled at the word fortress. At least it was an improvement over her previous word, a prison. He looked at the plain walls and ceiling as if seeing it for the first time. "I guess it does resemble a fortress in a way, but don't worry. It'll become home before you know it."

Not if I can help it, she said to herself.

"I was thinking it would be pleasant if we spent the day out together tomorrow," he said.

"Why?" she asked, startled out of her contemplation.

"Well, we are married, which means we'll have to start spending time together sometime. Besides, I don't think you're impressed with Cordia II. I want you to become more acquainted with it. See the good side of it."

"Okay," she agreed though she was doubtful there was a good side. It couldn't hurt to learn more about the place, she reasoned, and it would help wile away the time.

***

True to his promise, he was going to spend the day with her. They left immediately after breakfast.

"I don't know why where we're going is such a big secret," she complained.

"It's more fun that way," he answered.

"For who?"

He only smiled in reply.

She eyed the spaceship as they passed by it. She was struck not only by its glossy dark red sheen in a world of white but also the fact that this was her only way to get back to Earth.

"You're not going home," he said it lightly and teasingly, but Kristin could feel her heart pounding in her ears as her eyes moved from the spaceship to Moz'us.

"What?" she asked.

"That's not the surprise."

"Oh," she said, calming down. "I didn't think it would be."

He led her on until they stopped in front of a sign and a gate. She could see that past it were cages. "Is this where we're going?"

"It is."

"I haven't been to the zoo since I was eight and on a class field trip," she said with a laugh.

"Well, I can guarantee you that these animals aren't like the ones you saw."

"No, I suppose not," she said, her interest rising.

Moz'us paid for them to get in with Cordian currency.

The first cage they came to had four lizard-like creatures, and they were hissing at each other as if engaged in conversation. "You know these look just like miniature dragons to me even though dragons are mythical."

"Well, they basically are. They fly, breathe fire, and love shiny things. The only difference would be that they don't get big, and they're much friendlier."

They went onto the next cage. She stepped back when she saw the creature. The furry, white beast looked like a winged monkey.

"Just like *The Wizard of Oz*," she said.

"The what?" he asked with a confused expression.

"Never mind."

"It's called a blonda," he told her. "It's the last one of its kind."

She studied the animal carefully as it flitted around its cage. It must have longed to soar in the open skies instead of being trapped in a confined space. She could definitely relate.

She went onto the next cage unable to bare the sad sight anymore. In the next enclosure was the biggest cockroach she had ever seen in her life, at least two feet in size, and worse, it was flying around in its cage. Did anything not fly here? It was a mottled green with a reddish head, and a silvery-like horn protruded from the top of its head.

"That's a holden," he told her.

"Do any of the animals roam free?"

"Because it's not their native planet, there isn't any place left for them to roam. They do much better in confined care. Of course, we keep pets similar to your cats and dogs. They thrive well on Cordia II."

***

"I have to admit. It's been a fun and interesting day," Kristin told Moz'us that night.

She had been afraid that this day had all been a ploy to romance and bed her, but she knew now that he was the genuine article. He was honest, and he worked hard, not only helping his father with his political matters but working on their nonexistent relationship. Not to mention, he seemed to like animals. He was only trying to befriend her for now, and he had succeeded.

She turned to look at him and knew that he was asleep by his deep breathing. She found herself gently stroking his cheek. Her hand recoiled once she realized what she was doing.

She would be leaving after eight more days now. The last thing she needed was for it to be anything more than amity between them, the last thing either of them needed.

Chapter 8

Moz'us cradled a cup of coffee. He had been intrigued by the drink that Kristin kept going back for multiple times a day. The first drink had been bitter, and he had wanted to throw the rest out but feeling bad about wasting it and still curious about why his wife would drink this stuff, he had finished off the cup. Now it had become his usual breakfast drink, although he doubted he could ever drink as much as she could, but he understood the addiction better.

He smiled as he thought of their excursion at the zoo. She had been reluctant at first, but she had quickly warmed up to the idea with an almost childlike enthusiasm. There were times when she had thick icy walls up with sharp points, not unlike some Cordian buildings, and he felt like he wasn't making any progress at all and never would, and then there were moments where he sensed a warm, caring woman lay behind those walls.

It made him want to get to know and discover that woman even more. As much as he was against the idea of arranged marriages because they could end loveless and because the Earth women didn't know what they were getting into, he had to admit that this one had potential. He was falling in love with her little by little, and he hoped that she was falling in love with him too.

His thoughts were interrupted by a knock on the front door. "Come in," he called.

It was Aq'ots, his teenage cousin come to visit. "How is married life treating you?" he asked with a sparkle in his eyes.

"It's okay," he answered.

"Just okay?"

"I like Kristin a lot."

He guessed the reason for his calmness and the hint of worry. "You have not yet consummated your marriage," he exclaimed.

"Shh," he said, looking to the bedroom, where Kristin was still getting dressed. He didn't want her to think he was sharing their personal matters with everyone, and he definitely didn't want his parents overhearing.

"No wonder you're too listless to get the door. Who could blame you?"

He frowned at him. He was almost ten years his junior and too frank about such matters.

"I think it is good for you to take it slow and gain her trust. You will be with this woman for the rest of your life, and you want to start on the right foot, but I doubt the ruling class will have your patience."

He didn't need to be reminded of that. It weighed on his thoughts constantly. He had to impress on Kristin the importance of not taking their command lightly. He could give her a couple more days to become used to the idea of their marriage but no more. They were not a violent people. No one had been executed in a millennia, but if the ruling class so chose, they could both find themselves locked away for the rest of their natural lives and many had.

"What are you drinking?" Aq'ots asked, interrupting his thoughts and bringing a slight smile to his face.

"Try some," he said. "It defies words."

***

Moz'us stared hard at her pizza. The family still had not grown used to all the things she ate, and the pizza was a new marvel. She handed him a slice so stuffed with sauce and cheese, it could barely stay on the bread.

He took it from her and was clearly working up the nerve to take a bite. Kristin appreciated the trouble he was going to, although pizza was hardly trouble, she well knew how hard it was to try food from another planet. She'd tried a bite of strange vegetation the other day, which had been so sour, she didn't know how they could stand it or if she could bring herself to try something else.

He carefully took a small nibble, and his face lit up with enthusiasm. "This is good! I mean it is good the first time you try it."

"You didn't think it was poison, did you?"

He grinned. "I don't know. The jury's still out on the coffee."

"Says the person who drinks it everyday now."

After they'd all eaten, Ix'els said, "Son, come take a look at my speech on the importance of science and functionality over everything else. I want your opinion to see if it will properly impress the masses."

"Sure, Father."

She had a feeling that Moz'us didn't appreciate those things as much as his father did but was willing to put that aside.

Kristin got up from the table to make a beeline for the bedroom as soon as they were gone. She didn't want to make small talk with his mother, but Es'a grabbed her gently by the wrist.

"I am so glad that you came into Moz'us' life. You're really good for him. He smiles and jokes so much more since you've been here."

"Well, I'm pleased I can be of some help," she said politely before continuing her escape.

Kristin couldn't say she wasn't surprised. Sometimes these people seemed so cold and reserved, excluding

Moz'us. Maybe she had misjudged the Cordians race, or at least Moz'us' family.

If it was true that she made him smile more than was his custom, she was glad for it. He did have a gorgeous smile. She shook her head as she climbed into bed. The last thing she needed to think about was Moz'us' smile.

***

Kristin was being shaken awake. She was startled to find Moz'us' face inches above hers. Recovering from the shock of his closeness, she sat up and saw that it was still early. "What's going on?"

"We're going to church."

"Church?" she asked disbelievingly.

"You don't know what church is? Maybe I have the wrong word. The place you go to worship Kralgiek."

"You had the right word apparently. I thought science and government was your god."

"Unfortunately, to most people here it is, but as you surely know, not everything can be explained by science. There is room for faith."

"Like what?" she challenged.

"Love for one thing."

"And?"

"And where you go when you die."

"So you believe in this Kralgiek god then?"

"I would not attend church if I did not. Some people believe His prophecies are coming true and that Cordia II is the new Cordia paradise our scrolls speak of, but I don't believe it and neither does our priest. It's not mandatory for you to attend and believe in Kralgiek, but I would really like it if you went with me."

She ignored the invitation. "So you have a Bible then?" she asked.

"Not the same as yours, but yes. We have ancient scrolls given by Kralgiek."

"What's your church like?"

"You've never been to church before?"

"Yes, but that doesn't tell me anything. Even if you told me you were a Christian, church could range from men sitting on one side and women on another to handling snakes."

"We're not Christians, we're Kralgiekians. Christ was your world, not ours, but we do have a savior, presumably the same one but with a different name, not unlike *The Chronicles of Narnia*."

She snorted. "You know about *The Chronicles of Narnia*?"

"We had to read some of your classic books in class."

"And yet you don't know *The Wizard of Oz*?"

He shrugged. "It's impossible to read all of your books and know all about your culture within the confinements of a classroom."

"What about *The Lord of the Rings*?"

He shrugged again.

"Your education is sorely lacking."

"To answer your question, I don't believe we do anything that you would consider to be out of the ordinary. No snakes or any other creatures within our church walls."

"I have news for you. I don't attend church on Earth, and I don't intend to start in an alien city. And you seem awfully insistent, are you sure this isn't a ploy to sacrifice me?" She teased, and yet...

"No human sacrifices, I promise. I would just really like you to come with me."

He was so earnest that she couldn't say no. "I guess I can go just this once."

***

A red-haired man, who was their priest judging from his fancier robes flecked with gold, stood before them to speak. For most of the service, he spoke in an unfamiliar language. As Kristin was the only who seemed not able to understand it, she assumed he wasn't speaking in tongues but in Cordianese.

He suddenly switched to English. "Kralgiek is a jealous god. He demands our sole attention and love. He is the only god as the prophet, Yon'on, revealed to us. Turn to Him."

He had switched back to Cordianese. She had a feeling the priest thought of her as a heathen, which probably wasn't far from the truth. That short bit had her wondering though: one god, who wants love and full devotion. It sounded familiar and presumably there was no contact between their cultures until recent times. Somewhere there was a seed of truth and a common origin point. She wondered if she had more in common with Cordians than not.

Chapter 9

Kristin came to the breakfast table, looking somewhat pale.

"Are you feeling alright?" Moz'us asked her. "You don't look so good."

"Gee, thanks," she said sarcastically. "That's what a woman wants to hear first thing in the morning."

Despite her show at sarcasm, not to mention the fact that she had ignored the question, her voice hadn't sounded too strong.

He stood up. "I think you better go back to bed and rest some more."

Instead, she collapsed to the floor.

Moz'us got to her first. She was breathing, but it looked as if she had a nice knot on her head from her fall, and she wasn't conscious. His father bent over her as well. "We had better move her to your bed."

Together, they lifted and carried her into the bedroom.

She didn't wake up during the move to the bed, but now she thrashed around as if in pain. He sat beside her, unsure of whether he should try to still her or let her thrash.

Cordia II didn't know sickness anymore. They'd had sickness at one point, but germs had basically been eradicated from existence. Cordians died of old age, and on rare occasions, of grave physical wounds. They didn't die from something so tiny that it couldn't be seen with the naked eye. They didn't suffer like this.

"Do you think she will recover?" he asked, the worry evident in his voice.

"Sometimes they do, son. I hope so."

"And sometimes they don't?" he asked, already knowing the answer. He had known about it from his Earth history class. Thousands upon thousands of people had died during epidemics from things like smallpox, the flu, and plagues, but somehow it hadn't seemed real, and it had never occurred to him that they could still get sick once they came here.

"Everything is in Kralgiek's hands," his father said, putting his hand on his shoulder. "It may just be a simple illness."

"How could this happen? She's not on Earth."

"She no doubt picked it up on Earth or from one of the other brides. Don't worry; you can't catch it. Germs are unique to the planet and sometimes species they inhabit."

Moz'us didn't care about himself. He would gladly be sick for her if he could. He just knew he couldn't lose her. He hadn't realized the full depth of his feelings until now. He couldn't imagine his life without her.

His mother came in with a cold, wet cloth, "I have heard this will sometimes help them in sickness," she explained as she placed it on Kristin's forehead. "I hope it is not an old wives' tale. I don't know what else to do."

"Get one of the Earth women," he said. "They'll know what to do."

His father left immediately without question on the errand.

The cool cloth had calmed her down and ceased the thrashing. He removed her sweaty hair off of her face and prayed.

His father was back with one of the women from earth in just a few minutes. She shook his hand. "I'm Ruth Pearson." She felt Kristin's face. "Has she had any other symptoms besides the fever?"

"She looked a little pale and tired, but I don't think so. She hit her head when she fell down."

"I am by no stretch of the imagination a medical doctor, but it seems to me that the unconsciousness may be from the fever. The cool cloth will help, but I suggest sponging her with cold water. You just have to try and keep the fever down. I have some Tylenol with me. When she wakes up, give her one and that should help get her fever down. If that doesn't take care of it, I'm really at a loss."

"Thank you for coming over," Moz'us said.

"You're quite welcome. I'm glad to be of help. I'm sure she will be fine."

His mother had already gone and gotten a bowl of cold water and a sponge before Ruth even made it out of the door.

Moz'us started sponging her immediately. His parents left him to the task. He stopped only to test her forehead. She did feel a little cooler, but she was still hot. He kissed her burning but wet cheek and continued sponging.

***

Kristin slowly opened her eyes. Moz'us was sitting next to her. He held a glass of water and a pill in his hand. "Take this."

She didn't have the energy to protest. She took the pill dutifully.

Once she got her bearings, she remembered this morning. "I passed out, didn't I?"

He nodded. "You gave us a scare."

"And you've been nursing me the whole day?" she asked, seeing that moonlight was already filtering into the room.

He nodded again.

There was something so endearing about him caring enough to nurse her and being worried about her. She squeezed his hand. "Thank you."

"I can't believe that was just a minor sickness," Moz'us said, hoping Kristin wasn't going to dismiss it completely. "I know I haven't had a lot of experience with people being sick, but it seemed pretty serious."

She shrugged. "What can we do about it? Take me to a doctor? They're not exactly plentiful around here. And going back to Earth is not an option, is it?"

"I guess not, but I still think you should be taking it easy," he told her, knowing full well that she had no intention of listening.

"I feel great now. Honest."

***

Moz'us and Kristin went on an errand. She wanted fresh air, and he didn't want her to go anywhere alone until he was sure she was truly well. A rare part was needed for the fancy household machine that washed the clothing, and they were attempting to track one down. It seemed even alien technology wasn't above breaking down.

"Thank you again for nursing me back to health," she said.

"You don't have to keep thanking me. It's what spouses do; they care for each other."

"That may be, but not every spouse would have done it." She remembered when her mom got cancer. Her dad had thrown himself into his work rather than staying by her side.

"You're not only my wife; you're the dearest friend I have ever had."

She didn't know what to say to that revelation. She was speechless.

"We are friends, aren't we?" he asked a trifle nervously.

"I've never had many friends," she answered honestly. Her family had moved around a lot when she was younger, and she had never been much for friendly small talk. She was too blunt a lot of times.

"I haven't either, not true friends, not friends you can trust completely and who will stick with you come what may. The price of being part of the ruling class."

"I can relate. My father's in politics, too. You feel like you can trust me that much?" she asked, her eyes softening.

"I know we see eye to eye."

"But in some ways, we're completely different," she argued. She was feeling a little guilty about the come-what-may part."

"Not in the ways that matter," he insisted.

He was so sweet. There was no denying that she would miss him when she left. "And yes, we're friends," she said, remembering his question from earlier.

He stopped in front of a store that could only be described as the junk shop of Cordia II. She walked around, looking, while he explained to the shop owner what they were looking for.

There was machinery in all states of conditions and machine parts everywhere, and they were not very organized. Half of the metal objects looked rusted and/or had lost their shiny metal sheen.

It didn't take her long to become bored, especially when she didn't know what half the things were. Her eyes went to the window, and she shuddered when she saw the man who had almost become her husband across the street, glaring with hatred as he looked back at her.

Moz'us joined her, holding a small metal piece in his hand. "He had what we were looking for." He pocketed it and took a step toward the door.

"Wait," she said, putting a hand on his arm. "Let's stay in here for a little while."

"Why?"

She sighed and gestured toward the window with a small tilt of her head. "It's him."

"We were bound to see him sooner or later. Why shouldn't we go about our business?"

"Well, for one thing, and don't take this the wrong way, but you don't look like you could hold up in a fight."

"Thank you for your concern, but I could defend myself if I had to, and he's unlikely to start a knock-down-drag-out fight, especially in the streets. We're a peaceful people by and large"

"Are you sure about that?" she asked with raised eyebrows.

"Pretty sure. We'll just pretend we don't even see him."

She nodded her agreement. Maybe he was right, and although she didn't know what fancy weapons Cordians might carry on their person, she could hold her own in a fist-to-fist fight.

Once outside, Moz'us put his arm around her waist.

"What are you doing?" she whispered a bit harshly.

"The last thing we need is for him to get suspicious about us and report back. We need to show that we're intimate with each other."

"And you can't—" before she could finish, his kiss had cut off her tirade, and worse than that, when his lips left hers, she couldn't even remember what her tirade had been about.

"Good, he went inside. That got rid of him," Moz'us said and walked on like nothing had happened.

She suddenly remembered what her tirade was about. "You can't just kiss me like that or show displays of affection with people watching."

"Is that a law on Earth?"

"Yes. I mean no. It's an unwritten rule. You should do your kissing in private."

"But we don't do our kissing in private."

"That's beside the point."

"I think we've satisfied his curiosity, so we need to do a repeat performance in public anytime soon."

She had four full days left before she would be leaving. She had to remind herself of that and not think about that quick but searing kiss. She couldn't afford to get involved with him as good a kisser as he was, and he was good.

Chapter 10

Moz'us couldn't stop thinking about the kiss from yesterday. He questioned if he had really thought it was necessary to kiss Kristin, or if it had simply been the chance he was waiting for to kiss her. As much as she had protested about public affection, he had a feeling that she had enjoyed the kiss as much as he had. He wanted to kiss her again, but he would wait for her to initiate it if it was at all possible.

Speaking of kisses, the wriggly white puppy in his arms was trying hard to lick him in the face. He hadn't been able to resist getting it. He'd had a similar one as a boy, and he thought Kristin might like it as like them, the only difference between an Earth dog and Cordian dog was on the molecular level.

People were basically either cat people or dog people, and he was convinced that Kristin was a dog person. He wanted to make her smile with the gift. Genuine smiles from Kristin were so rare that he treasured every one, and he hoped it would make her feel more at home here.

He hid him behind his back the best that he could as he went through the door. "I got you something," he told her right off the bat.

"A ticket out of here, I hope. Why did you get me a present?"

"Do I have to have a reason?"

"What is—" before she could finish her question, the yip answered the question for him and he brought him out.

"A dog? I hate to tell you this, but I'm deathly allergic."

"Allergic?" he repeated, the word foreign to him.

"Yeah, you know, allergies. Living or nonliving things that make a person sick for no good reason. Your body's overreacts to something that's not really dangerous."

He'd never known that such a thing was possible. Cordians were either exempt from that to begin with or had stamped it out along with actual illness. His heart sunk. The puppy hadn't been such a great present after all.

He had to take it back, but the puppy leapt out of his arms and took off toward Kristin, running helter-skelter. He jumped up playfully at her, yipping excitedly.

"It's my curse," she explained with a wry smile. "For some unknown reason, dogs love me."

She didn't voice it, but he could hear the 'and I love them'. It was too bad that she was allergic to them. She scooped the puppy up despite her allergies. "It's too bad I don't have any allergy medication with me. It is kind of cute."

"You know you haven't had any bad reactions yet," he pointed out.

Her eyes widened. "I guess I haven't. Maybe I'm not allergic to Cordian dogs."

"Do you want to keep him?" he asked. "I mean assuming the allergies don't come later."

"I guess I wouldn't mind having a mutt around. You can keep him."

He didn't like the way she said you. It made him feel like she wasn't planning on being around for much longer. His mother often told him he worried too much, so maybe he was seeing problems where there were none. He could tell she was starting to trust him, and he already trusted her.

***

That night, he found Kristin on the floor playing with the "mutt". There was no mask to hide what she was feeling. She was happy and carefree in that moment, and it made him smile. It was so characteristic of her to feign a hard exterior, but whether she liked it or not, she was soft on the inside. He hoped she had as soft a spot for him as she had for the puppy.

He shut the door back softly and knocked, knowing she would want time to compose herself and pretend that she only halfway liked the dog.

"I've been thinking of names. How about Zusie? After you," she suggested.

"Isn't that a girl's name on Earth?"

"It might be," she said, trying to sound innocent but failing miserably when she couldn't stifle a laugh.

"I don't think so," he said decidedly.

"We have to name him something."

"I'd prefer we not name it after me. How about Cordia 2?"

"Cordia 2? Let me guess that was the name of a dog you had when you were a kid, not very original. I still like Zusie." The puppy came over and put his paws up on Kristin's legs, wagging its tail. "See? I think he even likes it."

"How about Lassie then? It's got the same sort of sound."

"You know that show?" she asked, her eyes glittering with amusement. "You have some of the most obscure Earth knowledge possible. And isn't it a boy dog?"

"Yeah."

"Lassie was a girl and a collie."

"Well, I guess we'll have to keep thinking until we find a name we both like. I can tell naming our children is going to be fun."

"You can say that again," she said with a burst of laughter that sounded very tight.

"I know that you're keeping something a secret, but whatever it is, I could keep it a secret, and I would for you."

***

Kristin was taken completely off guard. It felt a little out of the blue, but she had noticed that he was starting to get to know her like she was getting to know him. For some reason, it terrified her. No one had ever figured her out so quickly or better.

She took his hand. It felt like such natural thing to do, despite her reservations. "I know you would." She paused momentarily. Did she really believe that? They had only known each other two weeks, and it wasn't that long ago she had thought of him as an enemy, but she knew in her heart that he was trustworthy. "But I don't think you would like my secret."

"Maybe not," he conceded, "but as I told you, I would keep it."

"That's a tall order when you have no idea what it is."
He didn't answer but silently and patiently waited for
her to decide if she wanted to tell him. She did want
to tell him. She was tired of trying to figure out how
she was going to sneak away from him when the day
came; it would be easier if he knew about it. He might
even agree with her plan, since he had been against
the idea of the bridal exchange. She took a deep
breath. "I am going back to Earth."

He looked at her incredulously. It was the last thing
he had suspected she could tell. "And how do you plan
on doing that?"

"The ship that brought the first shipment of brides is
leaving three days from now to get the rest of the
brides, isn't it?"

"Yes," he answered, not liking where this was going.

"All I have to do is sneak on it before it takes off. It's
as simple as that."

He looked a little shell-shocked, but it was plain from
his expression that he thought her plan of escape
could work.

"So will you keep your promise and keep my secret?"
she asked. As sure as she was that he would, she
wanted extra assurance.

He was slow in answering but firm when he did. "If
that is what you truly want, to go back to Earth, I'll
even help you."

It was Kristin's turn to be stunned. She couldn't ask
for a better, more supportive husband if she were to

search both Cordia II and the world over, assuming she wanted a husband. She only wished that she could take him back to Earth with her, but she doubted he wanted to leave his home and his parents, and without a career or a purpose, she didn't think she could be happy here.

***

Kristin noticed that she received a significantly less number of stares when she walked the streets now. It was clear that the Cordians were beginning to get used to seeing women from Earth. It could only work to her benefit. If anyone caught her walking when she went to the ship, they weren't likely going to pay attention to her.

Brittney leaned against outside of the house, looking mildly bored.

Kristin went up to her and wasted no time. "So are you going to go with me?"

She shook her head adamantly. "No."

"Why? Are you afraid of getting caught?"

"My husband really isn't so bad once you get to know him. I mean maybe I could have done better. Heck, maybe he could have done better but then again maybe we couldn't have. And I'm getting used to this place. You can't beat getting whatever you want to eat whenever you want to eat it. You should try to make a go of it."

"I have tried." She knew it was a lie. She hadn't really tried, but she didn't have to try to know she would be unhappy in Cordia II. This was her only opportunity to leave. She had to take it no matter how used to Moz'us she had grown.

"I am sorry to hear that. I hope your plan is fail-proof."

"Nothing is fail-proof, but sometimes you have to take risks."

"Maybe. Well, good luck then. You're going to need it."

"Get word to me if you change your mind. I'll be here at least one more day." She was somewhat disappointed to discover that she would be going back to Earth alone, but it was nothing new to her, being alone.

Chapter 11

Moz'us still couldn't believe that she was really leaving. A terrible ache occurred whenever he thought about it. He knew that they could be in all sorts of trouble if they were caught, which could make anyone's stomach twist, but he knew the ache didn't stem from that alone.

Yet, if they weren't caught, Kristin would be beyond the repercussions, and he could claim ignorance on his part. He just had to make sure she got on the ship without getting found out. He probably should tell her the penalty involved if they were discovered, but he couldn't doom her to a life of misery with him. He just had to make sure the plan succeeded.

However it turned out, he knew he wouldn't be allowed to get married again. Kristin would be the only wife he ever had. Cordian marriages were forever, unless he could prove that they had never consummated their relationship, which would be practically impossible without her being here.

He had always been the kind of person who looked forward to having children, so he was surprised that he didn't feel more regret about it. He supposed the truth of the matter was that he would miss being a parent, but he would miss Kristin more, and it wouldn't be fair to have any woman compete against her memory anyway.

His thoughts were interrupted by Kristin's return. "It looks like I will definitely be going alone. Brittney decided no."

"That's good," he said. "The less people involved, the less risk there will be."

She plopped down beside him.

"You don't have to go," he blurted out suddenly. It may have been a dumb thing to say, but it was heartfelt.

"I really do. It's not that this is such a horrible place, and you and your family have been wonderful to me, but I simply don't belong here. Look on the bright side though, you'll have the pick of the litter with the next shipment of brides, and you'll have a bride who wants to be here and will be more cooperative and easy to get along with."

He forced a smile. "I don't think you were that terrible." He didn't have the heart to tell her he couldn't get remarried. He didn't want anything to mar her happiness. "In fact, I think you were pretty great."

"You don't mean that," she said with a roll of her eyes.

He not only meant it, he thought she was more than great. He loved her. He loved her like a husband was supposed to love a wife, and she was going to be gone the day after tomorrow.

***

It was her last night in Cordia II, and she was outside watching the foreign sun set, and the three moons rise one more time.

Somebody came out of the house and joined her. She didn't have to turn around to know which of the family it was; it was Moz'us. Lately, she seemed hyper-aware of him. She could distinguish his footsteps, his breathing, everything, from other people's.

"That's one thing I miss about Earth," she confided as the colorless sun completely set, "the sunsets."

"I've heard that Cordia used to have the most beautiful sunsets in the universe. The sun was a brilliant orange and cast all sorts of pinks and purples and reds across the sky. I don't how true that really is. I imagine some of the older people are rather nostalgic for our home planet and miss everything this smaller planet doesn't have."

"That's right. You've never seen a colorful sunset, have you?"

"I suppose I technically have, but being an infant when we had to leave, I don't remember it."

She turned around to look at him, and he looked so sad. Maybe it was the talk of his planet's end. A piece of his hair that curled ever so slightly was resting on his forehead, and it was so tempting to her to slide it back into place; it was tempting just to touch his thick black hair. "There isn't anything more beautiful than a sunset with a full pallet."

He spoke softly and looked at her tenderly, "I don't know about that. I can think of at least one thing."

Perhaps it was the talk of sunsets making her feel romantic, or maybe it was something else entirely, but she couldn't resist pulling him into a kiss.

The darkness shrouded their kiss, making it far more private than their previous one. The longing she felt grew right in the pit of her stomach as they passionately explored each other's lips. No other kiss she'd ever experienced in her life could compare.

When they stopped to breathe, he took her hand and led her back into the house to their bedroom. As soon as the door shut, he pulled her against him to pick up where they'd left off. The bed seemed to have a gravitational pull.

She moved her hands to his waist to pull off his shirt, and then realized he wasn't wearing a shirt but a robe. She gave a small chuckle. "I've never had to remove something like this before."

"I'll show you how it's done." He grabbed the hem of her own robe and slowly pulled it up and over her head.

She repeated the process with his robe and gave a small gasp when she saw how built he was; he absolutely could have handled a fight. She had never seen his muscles before. Cordian clothes were fairly good at hiding that sort of thing.

She didn't get too long to admire as he moved them back into their former embrace, causing them both to fall back onto the bed.

"Are you sure this is what you want?" he asked suddenly, bringing it to a grinding halt. He even took the sheet and covered her with it, even though they both still wore their undergarments.

She couldn't help but smile. He was always the gentleman when by rights he should have been with her two weeks ago and when it was clear that she wasn't going to put up a fight. She didn't know how much good the gentlemanly act did though as the thin, silky sheet clung to her, making her form quite clear even under the covering.

"I'm sure, but are you sure this is what you want?"

"I'm sure," he answered in a husky voice.

Her breath hitched when she saw his blue-green eyes up close. Every time she had been in similar circumstances with men all she could see in their eyes was lust. It wasn't that she couldn't see desire in his eyes, she could, but there was something else along with it, something wonderful that she couldn't quite put a name to. It sent thrills and chills through her body. Moz'us was right. There were some things more beautiful than a sunset.

***

The sunlight streamed through the window. Moz'us reached out to feel for Kristin and felt only the rumpled sheets where she had slept. He sat up straight, panicked. She wasn't in bed.

He jumped up and ran to the closet. Her Earth clothes and her purse were gone. Only her Cordian robes and nightgown remained.

He pulled his robe on over his head as he ran. He ran as fast as his legs could carry him, which wasn't fast enough, to where the ship had been docked. It was as he had feared; the ship was already gone. He searched the skies for a trace of her. He thought he saw a small moving speck in the sky, but it could have just been space debris. Kristin was gone.

He swallowed thickly. He would have gone to Earth with her. He realized he had never actually told her that he loved her, but didn't she know? Hadn't last night been proof of that? He had been so certain that she loved him too.

Chapter 12

Kristin was huddled in the shadows of the ship away from the window. It had been easier than she thought to escape. She had expected to find locks, or at the very least, somebody guarding the ship. It had almost been too easy. The ship had lifted up out of the atmosphere, and there were no alarms sounding or ships following her.

The butterflies in her stomach were still there even after Cordia II was far behind her. Something about the trip just didn't feel right. She should be overjoyed about leaving, or even mildly pleased, but she couldn't shake the feeling that she had left something important behind.

Maybe it was the thought of what might happen to the agreement between Earth and Cordia II if the Cordians found out she was gone and what the people of Earth would do if they found out she was the reason Earth didn't have a clean environmental slate. She was sure that Moz'us could cover though; she wouldn't have left if she thought he couldn't handle the situation.

Every time she thought of Moz'us, feelings and memories welled up inside her. Last night had been wonderful, better than wonderful, breathtaking, but it didn't mean anything. She tried to tell her pounding heart that. She was trying to lie to herself, and she knew it.

It had meant a lot. It had been far from casual, or even a friends-with-benefits arrangement, but she had still been too afraid to stay. She was afraid to give up her life on Earth and she was afraid that their relationship wouldn't work out. Her relationships usually went sour after this stage. No, they always went sour. She wouldn't be able to take it if their relationship fizzled out. No, it was better to end things on a sweet note.

Her eyes fell on her wedding necklace, and she gently touched it. She hadn't been able to leave it behind. She didn't know why. She hadn't planned on leaving with anything that she didn't come with.

She was startled by a shrill yip. A white puppy came scampering out, and Kristin let out a small groan. Now there were two things she had brought back with her from Cordia II. She had no idea how that dog had managed to follow her to the ship and hide as a stowaway without giving himself away.

"Oh, well. How much trouble could you really get into?" she asked. "Moz'us is going to miss you," she said as she ruffled his ears. "Moz'us is going to miss me," she added softly, knowing instantly that it was true as soon as it came out of her mouth. "And I know I'm going to miss Moz'us."

That was what she had left in Cordia II she realized for the first time, her heart.

The ship came to a stop, signaling it had landed on Earth. She lifted the dog into her arms. She waited as the door opened. The sunlight was blinding. It had been so long since she had been under a golden sun; it was almost too painful to bear.

She looked around as she made her way around to the other side of the platform. There was a long line of women waiting just beyond the ship. There was only one thing to do now that her plan had succeeded and she was back on Earth, she had to get back onto the ship. She had to get back to Moz'us whatever the consequences were when the Cordians saw her emerge.

"Hey, you there! Get in line or get lost!" shouted one of the guards.

Kristin joined the line. As she was waiting, she noticed that the women all had papers in their hands, and they were showing it to the guard before they were allowed to get on. She was fairly certain this didn't bode well.

"Papers, please," said the brusque-looking guard. It wasn't the guard that had pushed her on before like she hoped it would be. "And as you should have been instructed earlier, there will be no taking of pets."

"Oh no, I must have left the papers at home."

"Sure you did," he said snidely. "No papers, no leaving the planet."

"Do I have time to go back and get them?" she asked, trying to hide her desperation. She was sure she could find a way to forge them if she was given half a chance.

The guard's response was to pick up his walkie talkie. "We have a situation here. A young lady needs escorting off the premises."

Two guards came, and she knew it was hopeless. They took her to the gate and let her go with a warning.

She heard the small buzzing sound of the ship taking off and watched as it disappeared completely. It was ironic. She had been taken against her will to Cordia II and now that she wanted to get on the ship, she couldn't.

She let out a small, dry chuckle. That was the life and luck of Kristin Harvey, she thought ironically. She had no choice now that the ship was gone but to accept her fate and go home.

She looked down at the puppy. He at least looked happy. "Well, I guess you'll get to see how humans live here."

***

She set him down as soon as she got home and went over to the answering machine. She pushed play. There weren't as many messages as she expected there to be for a missing person.

"Kristin, this is your father," he said gruffly. Kristin rolled her eyes as if she could mistake his voice. "You know I did what was best for the country. I assume you're still coming for Thanksgiving. Call me if you're not, so I know whether to set a place for you."

"Kristin, it's Ashley. I'm in Washington D.C. for the day. We should have lunch. If you don't call me back, oh well. I'll assume you either didn't want to or didn't get the message in time." She would have loved to have lunch with her old roommate if she'd been here.

"Kristin, this is Derek. I know I sent you undercover, but why haven't you checked in? Harvey, you'd better call soon or I'm going to send somebody to find you!"

"Vote Bill Hake into office. He will listen to the people. This means you. Call our office at 555-2393, and tell him where you stand on the issues. Bill Hake is not a fake." She shook her head at the stupid slogan and deleted all her messages.

Four messages and one was a recording. It was kind of sad really. She could drop off the face of the Earth, and had, and nobody would even know it. She would be one of those people they found rotting in their apartment a year later because nobody cared enough to check in on them.

That wasn't true though, at least not anymore. This dog would care, and she was sure Moz'us would care if he was still with her. On Earth, the only one who had noticed that she was missing was her workplace, showing where her life was tied.

***

"What's wrong?" Es'a asked, knowing something was wrong the moment she saw her son's face.

"Kristin, she's gone. She went back to Earth."

There was stunned silence as his parents took in the news. His father spoke first. "Do you still want her?"

"Of course I do, but what can I do without alerting the ruling class to the situation?"

"Well, I have connections. I could say I need to look the ship over for repairs, and you could use that time to get to Earth with it."

"You don't know what this means to me."

He looked over at his mother and squeezed her hand. "I think I do, son."

Chapter 13

Moz'us stepped out and warm, golden sunlight hit his face. As he looked up at the brilliant blue sky and took in the thriving green plant life, he couldn't get over how beautiful Earth was. He could see why Kristin would want to return.

He knew her address from looking at the contents of her purse. As he walked along the streets of the busy city, trying to locate the street, people were giving him strange looks. He looked down. It was no doubt the robe that was doing it. Most people didn't wear these on Earth, at least not in this time or place.

He decided he'd better get some new clothes, so he wouldn't stick out. He went into the first clothing store he saw.

"Can I help you?" asked a saleslady.

"I'm looking for a set of new clothes." He held up a hundred dollar bill of American Earth currency that his father had given him leftover from when the ruling class had been exploring the suitability of Earth for brides. "Will this cover it?"

She snatched it from him. "It sure will." She picked out the clothes for him and showed him to a dressing room.

He changed into the leather outfit and studied himself in the mirror. He hadn't seen many people out there dressed like this either. He went back out and said, "I don't think this is quite me."

She looked at his discarded robe with a puzzled look. "What is you?"

He looked around for inspiration and didn't find any. "I don't know. Something more comfortable. With a pattern maybe?" he said as he examined the solid black leather.

She looked around for something to fit the bill. Meanwhile, Moz'us noticed that an elderly lady's purse had slipped off her shoulder and onto the ground. He bent over to pick up it up for her. The woman screamed when she saw him.

She took her purse back and started hitting him with it. A man, who by his silver badge seemed to have authority, rushed into the store when he saw the scene through the store window.

"What is going on here?" the man demanded.

"He tried to steal my purse," the old lady said, pointing an accusatory finger at him.

"It's a misunderstanding," Moz'us said.

"Sure it is, buddy. You can explain it down at the precinct," he said as he clicked handcuffs around his wrists.

Moz'us was too stunned by the situation to try to explain further, and he didn't want to cause an interplanetary crisis by resisting Earth authority. He followed the policeman out in his new leather duds.

After they booked him down at the police station, he was put in front of a telephone. "You get one phone call."

Moz'us started to push in the numbers of Kristin's telephone number as he'd memorized that information as well, which was probably what he should have done as soon as he landed.

"You have to pick the receiver up first," the cop told him, not sure if he was being a wise guy or if he had some sort of mental deficit.

"Right," he said, turning a little red.

***

"Do you know how close I was to putting an APB out on you? I should have called them sooner, but it's not like it's the first time you've gone AWOL. This, however, was a long time even for you," Derek said so loudly that Kristin had to hold the phone away from her ear.

"I know, but I do have good information about how the exchange is going." She was an FBI agent assigned to making sure the aliens only wanted the brides and not to invade another planet.

"If you ever worry me like that again, Harvey, I don't care if you solve the biggest case the world has ever seen or will see, I'm going to embed one of those pet tracking devices somewhere on your person and you won't be able to be in the bathroom without me knowing about it."

"I'm sorry. It won't happen again." She was glad that she was on the phone where Derek couldn't see her smiling. Behind all the yelling, she could sense a genuine fatherly concern in her boss' voice. He had been worried about her. It was a relief to know that at least one person on Earth cared or noticed when she went missing. "I'll be into work in the morning and fill you in."

"You'd better."

Kristin flopped down on the couch after she hung up and realized there was stuffing scattered all over the floor.

"Bad dog," she said, shaking her finger at the puppy and picking up the tattered pillow. She wondered is she would have anything left before he got through with his puppy chewing stage.

He laid down and whined.

"You really are pathetic," she said as she scratched his ears.

The phone rang. She answered it, but before she could say hello, the person on the end of the line spoke first, "Kristin?"

She nearly dropped the phone. It sounded like him, but it couldn't be. "Who is this?"

"It's Moz'us."

"How in the world are you calling from Cordia II?" she asked, wondering if she had fallen asleep on the couch and was dreaming this.

"I'm not. I'm calling from a Washington D.C. police station."

***

Kristin had to hold back a chuckle when she saw Moz'us sitting and waiting to be released. He was in a bad guy sort of outfit that contrasted so drastically with the look of humiliation on his face. She quickly found his arresting officer.

"Why was he arrested, Scott?" Kristin demanded. She was well-acquainted with all the local officers and had worked with them on cases many times. Moz'us hadn't explained it to her on the phone.

"He says that he was picking up an old lady's purse, but she says he was taking it."

"If he says that's what he was doing, that is what he was doing. He is a genuine boy scout if there ever was one." If there was an interplanetary chapter of the boy scouts, she added to herself.

Scott snorted. "How did you get mixed up with this character, Harvey?"

"He's my husband," she confided in a quiet tone.

"Your husband!" he shouted in surprise.

"You don't have to tell everyone in the whole world." She wasn't embarrassed about it, but it wasn't exactly how she wanted to break it to everyone, and there was usually always someone from the bureau hanging around the station.

"I just don't believe it. I would have bet that it was a one in a million chance that Kristin Harvey would ever get married. You are the most career-oriented, hard-nosed agent the world has ever seen."

"You never have been very good at gambling. That's why you owe me and everyone else you play with more than your next paycheck."

He grinned. "Well, if you say he's honest that's good enough for me. You've always been a good judge of character, and I can see how a situation like that might happen especially with the way he's dressed."

After a little bit of paperwork, he was released.

"Thank you for rescuing me," Moz'us said once they were clear of the police station.

"You're not even on Earth for twenty-four hours yet and you're arrested as a purse snatcher. And I thought I had a hard time adjusting to another planet." She couldn't keep the laughter out of her voice.

"And all I was trying to do was find some normal Earth clothes."

She chuckled as she eyed him from top to bottom. "I hate to tell you this, but that's not normal."

"I'm starting to figure that out, and the woman at the store still has my money, so I guess it's mine now. That is a hundred dollars of your Earth money wasted. My father only gave me five thousand."

"You paid a hundred dollars for that? I hope it's genuine leather. The clerk saw you coming. You better not buy anything else without me there. I don't think you have a sense of our monetary system, or our fashion sense for that matter."

The police station wasn't far from her apartment, and it didn't take them long to get there.

"So this is where you live," he said, his eyes roving around her nearly destroyed apartment.

"It's not usually this messy, I promise. This is courtesy of your little present."

"How's the puppy doing other than destroying your home?"

"Oh, he's just fine. In fact, it seems the mutt is adjusting quite happily."

"Don't worry. I'll be here to help you now. Have you thought of a name for him yet?"

"It didn't seem right naming him without you, and dognapping was not a planned part of my escape. I don't even know how or why he decided to follow me."

He stepped closer to her. "I know. He would do anything for you and follow you anywhere."

"Are we still talking about the dog?" she asked, stepping a little closer.

"Are you glad to see me?" he asked hopefully, losing a little of his earlier confidence.

Rather than giving him verbally, she showed him with a kiss just how glad she was. When they paused for a breath, she said, "You know I don't think you wasted your money at all."

Before he could ask her what she meant by that, she shoved him into her bedroom and slammed the door shut behind them.

Chapter 14

This time when Moz'us opened his eyes, Kristin was awake and still beside him. He pulled her closer.

"I still can't believe that you're real and that you're here with me."

He laughed and then suddenly sobered. With a look of adoration, he told her, "I love you."

"I love you too."

His eyes widened. He hadn't been expecting her to return the sentiment, at least not in words. "Do you really mean that?"

She knew why he was surprised; she had left him. She took his hand and interlocked fingers, "I realized once I was on the way back to Earth that while I'm not completely sold on your planet, I'm one hundred percent sold on you. I tried to go back. I was so afraid that I would never see you again. How did you get here anyway?"

"I took the ship."

"Do you still have it?"

"I covered it in brush for the time being until we find a better hiding place or have need of it."

She switched subjects with a groan. "I don't want to get out of bed."

"Who says you have to?" he whispered, laying a kiss squarely on her shoulder.

"Derek would have my head on a chopping block if I didn't show up to work today. He wants to know all about the Cordians."

"Who is Derek?"

"My boss," she said, throwing back the covers and starting to dress.

"I'd like to go to work with you and observe Earth's working customs," he said earnestly.

"See that's exactly the reason I can't take you."

"What reason is that?"

"Saying things like Earth customs is going to make you stick out like a sore thumb, not to mention the only outfit you have is your Harley Davidson gear, not exactly appropriate for the office."

"I can pick something up on the way."

"The last time I checked, it wasn't bring-your-spouse-to-work day. How am I supposed to explain you being there?"

"You were supposed to be investigating Cordians, right?"

"Yes."

"Well?"

"I think we should keep your origins on the down-low for now. I don't think you want to be interrogated or locked up again."

"I can tell him I'm looking for a job."

"If it's so important to you to see where I work, I guess you can come along." She picked up a magazine and found a photo of a man in a suit and tie to show him. "You need something like this, and check the price of your clothes before you hand over a hundred this time."

"Got it," he said. "And don't worry, I saw the store on the corner. I can buy something and be back before you even finish getting ready."

He was true to his word, and she eyed the black suit and white tie. "You look much better than the model in the magazine."

"Thanks. Your air here is so clean and crisp and fresh," he commented.

"I suppose that means the exchange was successful."

***

The elevator slowed to a stop as they reached the floor Kristin worked on.

"Remember, keep your mouth shut. Let me do the talking," she said, shelling out last-minute instructions. She took a deep breath and hoped no one recognized that there was something different about Moz'us. He without a doubt looked the part.

Everyone Kristin and Moz'us passed stopped to stare. They were surprised to see her back at work and even more surprised to see a handsome man following her. They ignored the looks and went straight to Derek's office.

Derek was surprised to see someone with her too. He stood up from his desk and she introduced them. "This is Derek Forrester, my boss. Derek, this is Moses," she quickly added, thinking of the closest-sounding name to his real name.

Derek shook his hand, but the curiosity didn't disappear as he asked, "Is he relevant to the case?"

"No, he's my husband."

Tyler, Derek's office assistant, had slipped into the office on that sentence to bring the coffee he had wanted. Tyler started to have a coughing fit, and Derek pulled at his collar as if he were having the first signs of a heart attack.

Derek regained his composure first. "I suppose this explains where you've been for the past two weeks."

"I guess it does," Kristin said.

"Why weren't we invited?" asked Tyler, looking somewhat hurt. He'd been like a kid brother to her.

She'd taken him under her wing as he had hopes of becoming an agent one day.

"It was a last minute thing, and it didn't take place in Washington D.C., but getting married wasn't the only thing I did. I went to Cordia II."

Derek turned a shade paler. "You went where? How?"

"All will be explained in my report. I have all sorts of information about their culture, and I can even say how brides are adjusting to their new home. Impressed?"

"Harvey, you never fail to surprise me. I want that report on my desk before the end of the day."

"That's not all I wanted to talk to you about," she continued.

"Should I sit down this time? I haven't even had my first cup of joe yet," Derek said, taking the coffee. "Tyler, I think you'd better get me a second cup."

"It's just a small favor," she said after Tyler was gone.

He reclined back in his office chair, resigned. "Well?"

"Moses would like a job here."

"Is this true?" Derek asked, taking a good, long look at Moz'us.

"Yes, sir," he answered.

"What makes you qualified?" he asked.

"I am a quick learner and an expert in technology. I think I would greatly enjoy keeping the country and the world safe."

There was a long, heavy silence, until at last Derek said, "I think we do have an opening in the computer science department. If Kristin thinks you can do this job, that's a high recommendation indeed. Her compliments don't come easily. Of course, it's not that simple. You must go through a background check and the like. The employment office is downstairs."

Derek offered his hand, and Moz'us stared at it, confused, until Kristin whispered to him that he was supposed to take it and shake it. Moz'us shot her a quick look of further confusion, but did as he was told.

"I'll show him around," she said. "I think he left his id in his other pants pocket though."

It was a simple request for Moz'us to have some id to begin the background check process, but it was one that he couldn't do. She realized that they needed help from someone who would understand Moz'us' background and would be willing to help him slip under the radar.

She remembered Senator Andrew Marks. He had argued that the aliens were coming in peace when people had been worried about abductions or world domination, and besides that, she had always liked the man. He struck her as one of the few honest politicians out there. He had appeared out of nowhere, a small town farmer from the Midwest, but it hadn't taken him long to become a national senator. The people loved him and for a good reason. If anyone could and would help Moz'us, it would be Andrew Marks.

Chapter 15

"Do you have an appointment scheduled with Senator Marks?" asked the secretary out front.

"No, but it is urgent, and I assure you Senator Marks will be interested," Kristin said.

"I'm sorry but no appointment, no seeing Senator Marks," she replied with absolute finality in her voice.

"I'm sure there must be exceptions to the rule," she retorted.

"He is a very busy man," the secretary said, raising her voice. "He cannot see every Tom, Dick, and Harry."

"If you just let us talk to him for five seconds, I—"

The senator must have heard the argument because his office door opened.

"I'll be happy to see these people," Mr. Marks said.

As they followed the senator into his office. Kristin took the opportunity to send a told-you-so look at the secretary.

Moz'us shook his head at her in a bemused way, but he should have been proud of her; she had resisted the childish impulse to stick out her tongue.

Mr. Marks went around to his side of the desk and waited for them to take a seat. He had such a warm, genuine smile that it buoyed her confidence. He didn't seem the least bit upset by the disturbance. "How may I help you?"

"I'm Kristin Harvey," she said, introducing herself.

"I can't give interviews right now if that's what you're after."

"No, I'm not a reporter. I work with the FBI. This is my husband, Moz'us. I was hoping you could help him."

"I certainly will if I can. What sort of help?"

"He's not exactly from around here," she explained.

"You mean he's an illegal alien?"

"In the very literal sense," Moz'us said, speaking up.

"You're from Cordia II?" he asked, his eyebrows shooting up toward his hairline.

"Yes, sir."

"You plan on living here on Earth?"

"Yes, that's what Kristin wants. I feel I can adjust to here better than she can to my planet."

"Well, seeing as how you're married, there shouldn't be a legal problem, and with the success in the exchange, people shouldn't be harboring ill will."

"We were hoping to keep it low profile if we can," she said. "You know the prejudice he would face, and we don't want our privacy taken away because people are busy studying him. And to work together, he has to be a citizen and have a background to be checked."

"So you want to work at the Federal Bureau of Investigation, full of people whose job it is to uncover secrets?"

"When you put it that way, it might sound a little crazy," Moz'us said, "but the job sounds like something I might enjoy, and I want to be with my wife. With Kristin's help and yours, sir, if you lend it, I'm sure that I can make it work. I know I would be an asset to the country. Otherwise, we may have to return to Cordia II if my real identity were to leak out."

"You seem to be a fine young man, polite and intelligent, and I wouldn't want to be a reason an American citizen couldn't stay on their own planet. It would be an honor to make your life on Earth easier."

Andrew began writing down some information on a notepad. He spoke at last. "I will make the arrangements, so that it appears as if you are my brother's orphaned child."

"You have a brother?" she asked.

"I did. He and his wife died in a car accident. You'd be surprised how easy it is to get some paperwork and pictures to make it seem like they had a child."

Kristin and Moz'us tensed when someone else entered the room. It was a graying brunette with a smile equal to the senator's. "I didn't realize you were having a meeting. Joan told me it was okay to come in," she apologized.

"That figures," Kristin muttered.

"It's no top-secret meeting, dear. In fact, it concerns you too, so it's really good that you're here. This is my wife, Lynn Marks."

Mrs. Marks shook their hands.

"Moz'us is from Cordia II, and Kristin is from Earth," Andrew explained. "They're one of the married couples from the exchange, and Moz'us wants to try living on Earth, and in order to do that successfully—"

"He needs a background, a history," Lynn finished.

It was easy to see that Mrs. Marks was a sharp lady and probably could have been in politics herself.

"Exactly, honey. I was thinking we could say he was our nephew and provide a few false papers and pictures. Would you mind going along with it?"

She turned to Moz'us and Kristin. "I know my husband is a good judge of character, and you look like sweet kids. I'd be happy to help."

"Well, it looks like you will be Moz'us Marks," Andrew said.

"Moses Marks officially," Kristin said. "I think it would be good if he had a name that sounded like a normal Earth name."

"Do you have a preference for a middle name?" Andrew asked.

"Not really," he answered with a shrug.

"What about Carter?" Lynn suggested. "That was my maiden name."

"Moses Carter Marks. I like it," Moz'us approved.

"I hope you know I wouldn't bend the law for just anybody, but there are some things and people worth protecting. This is a case of special circumstances," Andrew added.

"I understand, sir. I really appreciate what you're doing for me," Moz'us said. "If there is anything I can do for you, just let me know."

"You know I wasn't too sure about coming to your people's defense at first. I didn't know if another world would have the same morals as we do, but I decided everyone deserves a chance, and I got some gentle persuasion from my wife. Nonetheless, I was taking a risk. I'm glad you've proven to me that it was the right choice to make."

Moz'us smiled at the couple, and they smiled at him.

"You know," Kristin said as she looked back and forth between them, "you almost look like you could be a real family."

"Feel free to drop in on us anytime," Andrew said. "After all, we are your uncle and aunt now."

"Thank you again, Mr. Marks, Mrs. Marks," Moz'us said. "It means a lot. I like the idea of having a family on Earth."

"That's Uncle Andrew and Aunt Lynn to you," Lynn said.

They walked Moz'us and Kristin to the door and exchanged goodbyes at the door. "Goodbye, Moz'us. Goodbye, Kristin," the couple called.

"Goodbye, Uncle Andrew, Aunt Lynn," Moz'us said, trying the names out on his tongue.

Kristin had to restrain a chuckle at the shocked and mildly embarrassed secretary.

Once they were outside, Kristin asked, "Well, Mr. Marks, are you ready for your first day of work?"

Chapter 16

"I still can't believe it," Kristin said as they walked home from work and saw a truck expelling particularly obnoxious fumes. "I realize that people have cars and things that they can't afford to give up overnight, but there should be more measures being taken for a future without pollution."

"Your workplace makes sure your country stays safe?" he asked still trying to understand.

"Yes, at least, it's one cog in the machine. Peace has to be protected, especially in a free society. So did you enjoy your first day?"

"I have to admit that I did. It took me a little bit to get the hang of your earlier forms of computers, but to know that I'm helping to keep the peace as you say, it really feels like we're making a difference."

"Do you think you're going to like living here?"

"I think so."

Kristin suddenly experienced a strange sensation like someone or something was prying into her mind. For a split second, she wondered if Moz'us had a hidden power, but she knew he would never purposely invade her private thoughts even if he could, and when she looked at him, he looked just as confused as her as if he was experiencing the very same thing.

Moz'us' eyes widened as he figured it out. "It's a telepathic tracer! They are after us! They must have had another ship."

"How? What is a telepathic tracer?"

"It's a bit like the bloodhounds of your world. It is used to track criminals. Except they pick up on thought patterns rather than scents."

"Let's try not to think about anything then."

"Kristin, that's impossible."

"So what can we do?"

"Nothing but wait, I'm afraid."

He took her into his arms and held onto her. She could sense the intrusion into her mind getting stronger and stronger. She felt like a convict. She was afraid of what they would do to her and Moz'us. For all their advancements, they were not free of barbaric notions like bridal exchanges. She could hear her heartbeat getting louder and louder in her ears.

At last, the robed men and their flashing, handheld machine loomed in front of them.

"You are both under arrest," said one in a severe tone.

***

Kristin and Moz'us had been bound and taken back to Cordia II. Their captors hadn't said anything else to them after telling them they were under arrest even on the ship. Kristin didn't know if it was good or bad, but it didn't take them long at all to get a speedy trial. They were put before the ruling class as soon as they arrived at Cordia II.

Es'a, Ix'els, and Aq'ots gathered around them for moral support as soon as they were brought into the large room.

"I warned you that there was danger of this happening," Aq'ots said to Moz'us.

"You knew that there was this sort of danger involved, and you didn't tell me?" Kristin asked.

"I knew, but I thought you would be beyond their repercussions on Earth, and that I would face the heat alone here. I ended up following you, but I really thought they wouldn't pursue."

"It isn't noble, Moz'us, that you were going to face the firing squad alone. It's just stupid. You should have told me, and I would have definitely stayed." She turned back to his family. "What will they do to us if we're found guilty?"

"At worst, you could be locked up for the rest of your lives," Ix'els explained.

"And at best?" she asked.

"A shorter term," he said.

Kristin and Moz'us had special seating arrangements, being that they were the accused. The room was much darker than she expected. Lights were shone on the table of judges, and there was a single solitary light for whoever happened to be testifying at the time. It was designed to provide fear and intimidation. How did these five members of the ruling class hold the power over their life for something as simple as choosing where they lived? This was not an advanced society, no matter what kinds of technologies they had.

The good news was that Ix'els was one of the judges despite his personal involvement. Cordians believed that they could make decisions without letting their emotions get involved. Kristin knew they greatly overestimated the power of logic over emotions. However, the other four other judges did look cold and unfeeling.

The lead judge spoke. "We are here to determine the guilt of Moz'us and Kristin of Earth.

Chapter 17

"Moz'us, take your place."

He went up to the seat wearily. There was no swearing in, but there appeared to be some sort of lie detector, making the swearing in pointless.

The lead judge also handled the questioning. "Did you willingly leave Cordia II to go to Earth?"

"Yes," he answered.

"Were you planning to come back?"

"Yes," he answered again.

"To live or only visit?"

"We hadn't decided that far ahead."

"Was it to bring back your runaway wife?" he asked.

This was harder to answer because to say yes would be to incriminate her. "She tried to get back to Cordia II without success. She couldn't get the ship turned around, and her people would not let her get onboard again."

"Why was she on the ship in the first place?" He looked toward her shadowed figure, and she nodded to encourage his truthfulness, not that there was a choice with the lie detector in place.

"She wasn't sure what she wanted, but now she is."

"Thank you, Moz'us, that will be all."

Kristin was amazed to find the questioning over so quickly. There was no beating around the bush with them. He came back to his original seat beside her and squeezed her hand reassuringly as her name was called to come up.

"You left Cordia II even after you agreed to be a bride, didn't you?"

"I didn't agree to be a bride as I've tried to tell you people from the beginning. I was kidnapped."

"Just answer the question, please."

"Yes, I left Cordia II."

"Have you been intimate with your husband and only your husband since coming here?"

Kristin's eyes widened. This was an unusual line of questioning and not relevant to whether they intended on returning to Cordia II, unless they were trying to prosecute her for not being a good wife as well. "I don't see how that's any of your business."

"Answer the question or we will take the answer to be no."

She just wanted this to be over. "Yes, I've only been with my husband."

"Were you going to return to Cordia II?"

"If Moz'us would have, I would have. As much as I love my life on Earth, I love him more."

"That will be all."

Es'a was called to the seat next.

"Was she happy in your household?"

"It's only natural that people need time to adjust to new circumstances."

"Was she happy in your household?" he repeated.

"No, but she liked us, and she loves my son."

"Do you believe that she could ever be happy in your household?"

"I believe that a person can learn to be happy anywhere."

"A wise answer, Es'a, but if she does not learn to be happy and attempts to return to Earth again, would she take any offspring garnered from the union and would Moz'us follow?"

"I really can't speak for other people."

"You are here to be a character witness and provide some insight into the possible future. Take your best guess."

"I would guess then that she would never keep her children away from their father, and Moz'us would do his best to preserve their union as would she. He would follow her, and she would follow him. Hence, they would be happy together whether they were here or on Earth. If they are required by law to stay here,

Kristin will obey the law if for no other reason than to protect Moz'us. "

"That is sufficient."

Kristin wasn't taken by surprise to hear them call Renee to the stand, and she knew it didn't bode well.

"Is it true that the accused, Kristin, approached you on two separate occasions?"

She twirled her hair nervously. "It's true."

"And also that her mission was to convince you to return to Earth with her?"

Kristin sighed deeply. There was no way to sugarcoat this answer. It wouldn't look good to the council member that she had tried to talk others into committing this so called crime.

"Yes, but she would never have forced me. She was only concerned for my happiness here."

"That will be all."

Kristin knew it was looking pretty bleak despite the efforts of Es'a and Renee to make the truth look better than it was. There was no proof that she and Moz'us intended to come back or were even thinking of coming back, not that Kristin wasn't hoping that Moz'us would be happy on Earth and never want to live in Cordia II again.

Both Moz'us and Kristin were downright astonished to see Andrew and Lynn Marks come into the courtroom with an escort. Both of them shot them reassuring smiles to let them know they were here to help.

"I can't believe they got witnesses from Earth."

"They can be harsh in their punishments," Moz'us told her, "but they are fair and thorough. I don't know how they found out about them so fast."

Andrew was called to the stand first.

"How do you know the accused?"

"They came to me seeking help. They wanted a cover for Moz'us."

"In other words, they were seeking to stay on Earth permanently, and Moz'us needed an alternate identity, so that he could fade into the background."

"That's not the impression I got from Moz'us. I gathered he wanted to learn a little about the home of his wife first without drawing a lot of unwanted attention."

Despite the lie detector, most of the council didn't look as if they were ready to swallow that.

"Can you tell us why you are so eager to help this alien as your people would call Moz'us? Could it be that you want our secrets for yourselves?"

"I object! He is leading the witness," Kristin called out, gathering an affirmative nod from Lynn.

"This isn't a courtroom on Earth. You have no right to object," the head judge told her.

"We have helped and continue to help," Andrew answered, "because it's the right thing to do. I was raised to believe that we are put here to help our fellow man, no matter where he's from. If Moz'us had proven to me that he had criminal intentions, of course the story would have been different, but I hope that if I was in similar circumstances, there would be someone to help me out."

"That is all we wish to know from you, Andrew Marks, you may get up."

Lynn didn't do much more but affirm Andrew's testimony.

She was the last witness, and there was a quiet discussion among the judges.

Speaking at last, the head judge asked them. "Before we can make a final ruling, we must ask, do you plan on escaping Cordia II again?"

"No," she said, trying not to think of all they lost by being here, including their dog, which was still back on Earth.

"We have taken into account that she carries the first known offspring of our new mixed race."

Kristin and Moz'us gasped. She remembered that they had ran a small machine over her after their arrival they hadn't done the first time. She had assumed that it was some kind of security check even though they hadn't done it to Moz'us. She didn't know it had told them that she was pregnant.

"You will both be under house arrest for one year. If you leave the premises at all, it will be with a guard. "

It wasn't an ideal sentencing, but she was thankful it wasn't a lifetime of incarceration.

Chapter 18

Kristin looked down at her bulging belly. It had been a little over nine months, and she was going stir crazy, both because of the house arrest and because her due date had passed a week and a half ago. She sat down in a chair facing the window, her only link to the outside world, unless you counted their guard, Ras'on, as a link to the outside, which she didn't.

The puppy now almost full-grown nuzzled her hand, and she stroked the top of his head. The council had made a special trip just for the dog, not wanting even an animal from Cordia II to stay on Earth.

Kristin and Moz'us had finally decided on a name. Hopefully, they thought of a name for their child with less hassle. It was corny, but it seemed to fit, Apollo, after the first mission to put men from Earth onto the moon. He provided some comfort and distraction during their house arrest.

"I know you're miserable," Moz'us told her softly, crouching down beside her.

"I'm not miserable." She saw the disbelieving look he gave her. "At least, not completely. It's just this society of yours; it's not for me. I realize that in another few months I will be free to go outside, but what am I going to do with myself? What can I do with myself? It won't be much different from this stupid house arrest.

"Don't get me wrong, Moz'us. I don't mind being stuck in here with you, and I know that soon we'll have a child, who I will love and will likely keep me busy. It's just… this sounds selfish, but I need to work. I have to work. I need to know that I'm doing something productive and important outside the home."

"If I could make it any better for you, I would."

She smiled and touched his cheek. "I know you would."

"I'm going to do it," he said suddenly. "I don't know how, but if I can't talk them into letting us go back to Earth then we can change things here. We will change things here."

Kristin was surprised by his sudden determination. "Careful, Moz'us. You may get more time under house arrest."

"It's worth any risk. In fact, I think I might have an idea, but I don't want to make any promises."

A look of great distress crossed her face.

"Of course, if you don't want me to…"

She shook her head, her lips tightly pressed. "It's not that. I think it's time." She looked down. "I know it's time."

He helped her stand up and walk to their bedroom.

"You wait right here. I'll get help," he instructed once she was safely lying down on the bed.

Kristin rolled her eyes. She was in labor and under house arrest. Where was she going to go?

Moz'us was back in record time, and he brought Es'a with him.

"Do you want me here during the birth?" she asked.

Kristin smiled. "Of course, I do." She was grateful to have someone who had been through this before with her, and she knew how much it would mean to the kind woman to be there for the birth of her grandchild.

"Ras'on went to get medical help," Moz'us explained.

"Quick, this is our chance to escape," she joked before another contraction took hold of her.

It didn't take long for the birth attendee, as they called them, to arrive. After a quick examination, he told Moz'us, "The birth is proceeding naturally for one of her species."

The birth attendee took a step back from Kristin when he say her fist. She was ready to hit him for making a comment, which made her seem like an animal. The only thing that saved him was that she was in too much pain to get up.

The birth attendee spoke something quietly to Moz'us, sensing that another comment in the moody mother's hearing would likely not end well.

"What?" Kristin demanded.

Moz'us cleared his throat. "The heads of the ruling class, not including my father, of course, waits outside the house. They would like to witness the birth in person."

"Excuse me?"

"You see, this is a momentous occasion to them. It has historical significance. It'll be the first child of both Cordian and Earthly heritage."

"I am not having a bunch of old men standing around and watching this like it's some sort of a documentary or science experiment. I am not giving birth to a prince, and even if I were, I still wouldn't let them into the room. Tell them to forget it."

Moz'us left momentarily to inform the ruling class in a more polite way that the mother wanted privacy during her birth.

When he came back, the baby was finally ready to make an appearance. The birth attendee was preparing to catch the baby and telling Kristin that she needed to push. Es'a had one of Kristin's hands. Moz'us took the other. Despite the fact that Kristin's squeezing hurt his hand, he never let go, and it wasn't long before a crying filled the room.

The birth attendee cleaned the baby up and passed it off to the father. "I will go and inform everyone that the first child of both Cordia II and Earth is a son."

Moz'us brought their baby to Kristin. She felt a love cascade over her the moment the infant was placed in her arms. She didn't know what the future held for them, but she knew that with such a beautiful family, she could face life whether they ended up stuck in Cordia II for the rest of their lives or on Earth. Yet, she desperately hoped that Moz'us was able to succeed in whatever plan he was forming.

***

Andrew Ix'els, or Drew for short, stared up at his parents with his big wide blue-green eyes. He was named after Andrew Marks in gratitude of the help they had received from him both on Earth and Cordia II. His middle name was for his Cordian grandfather.

"How has this plan of yours to escape gone?" she tried to sound somewhat disinterested, but she couldn't keep the hope out of her voice, which was soon deflated when she saw his expression.

"Ever since we escaped, security has been too tight, and even if it were not, they would simply track us down on Earth again."

"So what you're saying is that there is no way for us to escape."

"There's only one way."

She didn't dare to hope again. "And that is?"

"Through the ruling class."

She was glad she hadn't gotten her hopes up again. "It would be easier to convince a cat to swim."

"I did appeal to them, and there's more of a chance than you think with my father being one of the ruling class—"

"Who, no offense, wasn't able to keep us from getting under house arrest. It was sweet of you to try though, so thank you."

"We'll see, but I've already gotten them to concede on one point."

"What point?"

"We don't have much of a need for keeping the peace here, but they are willing to put you in charge of documenting history, or in other words, running a newspaper. You will get to record daily events in your words and share them with the people of Cordia II."

"I get to express my opinion and have freedom of the press?" It was a step toward a free society.

"As long as they approve."

"I love this place," she said sarcastically. "It's like living in the dark ages with technology."

"We can bring change here," he insisted.

"That's unlikely. Most of your people are slaves to tradition and science with a prejudice against people from Earth, and seemingly women, since there are none at the judge's table."

"What if you had lived on Earth before things began to change for women? Would you have still found a way to make a difference?"

"Of course, but—"

"Use that determination to make the changes needed here. You already have an opening. You may not be able to blatantly express your opinion, but you can do it in more subtle ways as you write. It probably won't happen right away—"

"I know it won't happen right away."

"But I know you can do it. We can do it together."

Chapter 19

"You're right about one thing. This city is due for some change. I suppose it is time to make the best of a bad situation," Kristin said, standing up.

"Where are you going?"

"I'm taking Drew on a walk. Now that our time on house arrest is up, I appreciate being away from these four walls."

"Am I invited on your walk?"

"I don't know. What do you think, Drew?" she asked the baby. He made a gurgling sound. She smiled at Moz'us. "I guess that means yes."

She placed the baby in the stroller, and they proceeded to head toward the front door. The stroller was a lot like a stroller from Earth except it was made of a clear material to allow the baby to study his or her surroundings more fully.

"My little Andrew," Es'a cooed when she saw him.

"That's Drew Ix'els, dear," said the proud grandfather, who was also leaning over the stroller to greet the baby.

Kristin smiled at the doting grandparents.

"You should think about taking him before the ruling class," Ix'els told them. "They are still eager to meet the first baby born of both Cordia II and Earth."

"We'll think about it," Moz'us said though he knew what her answer would be.

The stars were making an appearance, and Drew seemed fascinated. There was no denying he was a curious baby.

"I suppose the stars here are beautiful in their own way," she said, "though they're nothing like the constellations on Earth. Just imagine, Drew will probably never see blue skies, never see yellow sunlight. It's a shame, but maybe it's better that way, not to know what you're missing. There's so much about Earth I took for granted."

"You do have a beautiful planet," he agreed. "I kind of miss it myself."

There were other mothers out with their babies, some fully Cordian and a couple newborns of mixed heritage.

"You know my father is right about taking him to see the ruling class in an official capacity. It might make them friendlier in the future."

"I'll think about it. I still can't believe they thought I was going to let them witness the birth. Maybe if they spent more time doing their job and less time witnessing births, they would be more fair-minded by now."

"You certainly know how to hold a grudge, don't you?" he asked with amusement.

"Not always. I might be willing to forgive them if I wasn't being held captive. In fact, I think I already have an idea for my first piece."

"Do I want to hear it?"

"Probably not." She gave a deep sigh of satisfaction. "I can't wait to get started writing."

"One thing they can't fault you for is honesty. Don't forget they have to approve it."

"I remember," she said mysteriously.

✶✶✶

"What are we doing?" whispered the Cordian boy beside her. Her young assistant reminded her of Tyler. She missed the pesky kid following her around at work. She also missed Derek and his badgering. A situation she hoped to rectify soon.

"Shh, we're reporting," Kristin whispered back.

Aq'ots was on her other side. He thought the enterprise interesting and had asked to come along. "I thought it might be something more along the lines of stalking."

"If anyone in the ruling class has skeletons in their closet, we won't know unless we see it for ourselves. They're not going to up and confess it to us in an interview. Being a good journalist mean going behind locked doors, and yes, doing a little spying at times."

Aq'ots grinned. "I know. I was teasing. Still, it's a good thing my cousin isn't here. He might be a little uncomfortable with the situation."

Moz'us was spending time with the baby, and Kristin had purposely excluded him from the outing, knowing what he would think of what they were doing. "I'll tell him all about it when we've made a little progress."

"Wise decision, boss," Aq'ots said, obvious amusement in his voice and probably on his face if there had been enough light to see it.

Aq'ots, Stok'ains, and Moz'us made up the team of people that worked under her in this Cordian newspaper project. It had been six weeks, and they had yet to make the splash she hoped to make. It had been all filler, fluff pieces, no corruption or scandal exposed yet.

After a month they'd called her before them to tell her what a fine job she was doing. They'd also been pleased when she finally took Drew for them to see. It was throwing them off guard, and she was gaining a slow following among the people of Cordia II, who were interested in the paper, so maybe all the pleasant pieces hadn't been a complete waste of time.

Kristin was about to call it a night. Picking up good leads and stories in Cordia II seemed practically impossible. It always ended as cold as the culture.

They had been watching the place for two and a half hours with no result. He had come home from work and done nothing but eat and read. This judge was up to nothing incriminating, at least not tonight.

Before they could get up to leave from their crouching positions, however, a woman came to the door. She was a lot younger than the councilman. He seemed to have been expecting her as he quickly let her into the house. It became apparent that it was no family relation once the door was shut.

"Where is his wife?" Kristin whispered.

"She stays with her daughter sometimes. I don't think she gets along with her husband as well as she could. Mind you, it's just gossip," Aq'ots explained.

"Clearly there's more truth than exaggeration to it. Do you know the young woman?"

"No, and I know practically everyone around here." Which is why she thought Aq'ots was right in pursuing this career path.

"Interesting. He's with a woman who isn't his wife. Do they frown on that in your culture?" Kristin asked.

"They don't applaud it," he replied.

"So you think the woman is from Earth?"

"It isn't a woman from Cordia II," Aq'ots said. "Look at that necklace she's wearing. We don't make necklaces like that here."

"I believe we have a story."

Stok'ains was astounded. "You're going to put this in the paper?"

"I don't know yet. That depends on the cooperation we receive from our upstanding, straight-laced judge."

Before he could question her further, Kristin had gone over and was knocking on the door.

They could hear the sounds of scrambling as the woman left the front room before the door was answered.

The judge clearly tried to maintain a calm composure, but he couldn't erase the guilt off his face completely. "May I help you?"

"It seems we've stumbled onto an interesting story," Kristin said. "I wouldn't necessarily divulge it, but-"

He got the message, "And what price would I pay for your silence on the matter?"

"Being a better husband to your wife for one thing," Kristin said.

He nodded, relieved at the terms thus far. "I can do that."

"And since you clearly are less prejudiced against the people of Earth than I was originally led to believe," she continued, earning her a fierce glare from the man, "I believe that women from Earth should be allowed to visit our home planet once in a while."

He shook his head. "Out of the question. The others would never go for that."

"I can guarantee that Ix'els would back you."

"I'm sure he would, but you could never win the others over."

"I couldn't, but you could," she said.

"Who would take the word of an Earthling bride over a Cordian member of the ruling class? I think you are an empty threat. Your story won't make it to publication. Now why don't you run along home and stick to your stories about weddings and social events."

"In that case, I think Cordia II would like to know of your fascination with women of Earth. I think you also forget that I'm not the only witness. Two solid Cordian citizens also witnessed it. I think it would be a heartwarming story for the history records, whether it makes it past or not remains to be seen, but if it does, it would really show the future generations how our two peoples became one, or at the very least, it would show the judges."

The judge cleared his throat. "I think we can figure something out."

Chapter 20

"Ambassador, nine months on Earth and three months in Cordia II. I still can't believe they agreed to it," Moz'us said, "especially with our record, but I told you to have faith in people."

"You were right," she agreed, keeping her eyes on the road and the smile under wraps.

"The question is if I should continue with my Moses Marks persona." There were a lot of things to consider now that they were on Earth again.

"I think you should. Even ambassadors need the peace and quiet that comes from anonymity."

"You sound like you know about having dual identities."

"I have gone undercover, and I know from my job experience that people can often miss what's right in front of their own noses, which can only work to our advantage. Most people will be so thrilled that you're protecting the Earth, but others will treat you like a celebrity or with suspicion. Dual identities are the only way to go."

"Are you going to be okay with the three months?" Moz'us asked.

"I am. Now that I'm not a prisoner, I can see the beauty of Cordia II. I still think it could use some change in how they view women, particularly ones from Earth, but I think I'll enjoy those three months. It was nice of Ot'eon to argue so hard in out favor, was't it?"

"I don't get that either. He's probably the most hard-nosed of the bunch. Why did he suddenly have a change of heart?"

"Let's just say he had some gentle persuasion."

Moz'us looked at her warily. "Do I want to know how you did it?"

"It's not that bad, trust me. Let's just say sometimes it pays to be a detective."

Apollo whined for some attention as Kristin parked the car on the side of the street. Moz'us reached back to pet him.

"Speaking of houses," Moz'us said as he unbuckled their son.

"Which I didn't know we were but go on."

"We need to find a place."

"You're right," she said as she pushed the elevator button.

"I can't wait for your father to meet Drew. I bet he'll be surprised."

"He'll be surprised alright, but I'm sure not half as shocked as my coworkers will be."

Her prediction was proved right in a matter of seconds.

Tyler's eyes widened when he saw them step off the elevator. "Kristin, you're back, and you're a mommy?" he queried in the same breath.

She chuckled, "Believe it or not, Tyler, I've missed you, and yes."

One of her other coworkers snorted. "You're gone then you come back with a husband. You're gone again, and you come back with children. What are you going to come back with next time, Harvey, grandchildren?"

"I'll come back with a train of orphans if I want to, Jerry."

He snorted again and went on about his business.

Kristin looked at Tyler again. "If Derek doesn't blow his top at the time I've been gone, maybe we'll be working together again."

"Are you kidding," Tyler said with a grin. "There's no way he'd let some other agency snap you up. I'll see you guys later."

They were about to test Tyler's theory. Moz'us knocked on Derek's office door, and they heard a "Come in!"

Derek sat behind his desk. "Kristin Harvey," he said in a gruff voice that belied the smile on his face, "why did I have a feeling that I hadn't seen the last of you?"

"Your investigative instincts I suppose," Kristin said her eyes full of joy and amusement at the greeting. She had missed the short-tempered older man more than she could say.

"I assume you're here to get your old job back."

"You would assume right."

"So you're gone for over a year, and you expect to come waltzing in here and get your old job back just like that?" Derek asked. "Give me one good reason why I should take you back."

"I can give you three. I've been living in Cordia II against my will, so it's hardly my fault that I couldn't report to work. Two, I've got more information than you can count as a result of my experiences, and Cordia II is going to let me spend three months out of the year to gather intelligence on the situation there. And three, you need me."

He pretended to think about it for a few moments and then said, "Okay, you've convinced me."

He seemed to notice Moz'us and the baby in the corner for the first time. "Is this your child? Has Moses been living with you in Cordia II?"

"Yes, this is Drew, and see some of that time I was missing, I would have been on maternity leave anyway. And yes, Moses snuck to Cordia II with me.

Derek walked over and took the baby in his arms. "I can already tell this kid's going to be as bullheaded as his mother. He's got your eyes and mouth. I wish you both luck with this one. Just remember what goes around comes around, Harvey."

Kristin chuckled. "I'll remember that."

"I suppose you'll want your job back too," he said, eying Moz'us.

"If you have room for me, sir," Moz'us answered politely.

"If I remember correctly, you're Senator Marks' nephew."

"Yes, sir."

"When can you two start working again?"

"Tomorrow, we hope," Kristin answered.

"I expect you both here bright and early, no excuses."

"Yes, sir," Moz'us responded.

"See that's another reason to keep Marks around. He gives me the respect I deserve. You could learn a thing or two from this man."

Kristin rolled her eyes and made a move to leave.

"Welcome back, Kristin," Derek said, becoming serious. "Things haven't been the same around here without you."

***

The early twentieth century townhouse had a distinct personality and character. Something she found a whole lot more valuable since Cordia II. The last thing she would have wanted was a home in suburbia. She marveled at the intricately carved stair rail, the charming fireplaces, and the fancy little window on the top floor, dead center in the house. No other townhouse on the street looked like it. She liked it, and she could easily picture living here.

"Do you like it?" she asked Moz'us, knowing it wasn't just her choice anymore.

"I love it, and it's in our price range. You sure this is the one you want?"

She gave the townhouse one last quick perusal with her eyes. "It is."

Moz'us stayed inside with the realtor, to discuss how to make it their home. She went outside with Drew still not able to believe how fresh the air was outside. She let Apollo out of the waiting car, so he could stretch his legs.

There were two small patches that served as a garden. Kristin had never been one for nature or gardens, but she had also developed a whole new appreciation for that as well. She reached to the ground to pluck a flower. She had never seen a prettier, more flawless daisy in her life. The clean air was already making the plants healthier.

Drew pulled the flower out of her hand and held it tightly in his fist. Kristin smiled as he studied it and then shook it to see if it did anything interesting. She had been worried that he would never get to see anything from Earth and now he was going to get to see and experience the best of both worlds and call them both home, a true gift in her opinion.

Moz'us and the realtor came out. She locked up the house and then left them to admire their soon-to-be new home.

"Are you sure you re going to be happy here on Earth?" Kristin asked Moz'us for what had to be the hundredth time.

"I'm positive. I love you, and I love your planet. It's going to be very fulfilling to work as one of you and as an ambassador. I think we're going to be able to make a difference on both Earth and Cordia II. This bridal exchange is the best thing that could have happened to us in more ways than one."

She agreed with him. She had everything: a loving family, a career, a home with a newly restored atmosphere. Together she knew she and Moz'us would make an unstoppable team in both worlds.

She truly thanked God that she was one of the green brides, or Moz'us' bride to be more specific.

The End